614

3800 18 0004983 9

HIGH LIFE HIGHLAND

D1464064

WITHDRAWN

SPECIAL MESSAGE TO READERS

THE ULVERSCROFT FOUNDATION
(registered UK charity number 264873)
was established in 1972 to provide funds for
research, diagnosis and treatment of eye diseases.
Examples of major projects funded by
the Ulverscroft Foundation are:-

- The Children's Eye Unit at Moorfields Eye Hospital, London
- The Ulverscroft Children's Eye Unit at Great Ormond Street Hospital for Sick Children
- Funding research into eye diseases and treatment at the Department of Ophthalmology, University of Leicester
- The Ulverscroft Vision Research Group, Institute of Child Health
- Twin operating theatres at the Western Ophthalmic Hospital, London
- The Chair of Ophthalmology at the Royal Australian College of Ophthalmologists

You can help further the work of the Foundation
by making a donation or leaving a legacy.
Every contribution is gratefully received. If you
would like to help support the Foundation or
require further information, please contact:

THE ULVERSCROFT FOUNDATION
The Green, Bradgate Road, Anstey
Leicester LE7 7FU, England
Tel: (0116) 236 4325

website: www.foundation.ulverscroft.com

THE PLOT THICKENS

The Archway Players are struggling this year to put a Christmas production together in their seaside Cornish town. Adam, a member of the troupe since he was a teenager, is distracted by Gwen, his would-be girlfriend. While Gwen, a health care worker who lives with and cares for her father, doesn't always have the time she needs for the production — or Adam. And when the lead actor is attacked and put in hospital, it looks as if the show might not go on — unless new ideas are found fast.

WITHDRAWN

CHRISSIE LOVEDAY

THE PLOT THICKENS

Complete and Unabridged

LINFORD
Leicester

First published in Great Britain in 2018

First Linford Edition
published 2019

Copyright © 2018 by Chrissie Loveday
All rights reserved

A catalogue record for this book is available
from the British Library.

ISBN 978–1–4448–4033–9

Published by
F. A. Thorpe (Publishing)
Anstey, Leicestershire

Set by Words & Graphics Ltd.
Anstey, Leicestershire
Printed and bound in Great Britain by
T. J. International Ltd., Padstow, Cornwall

This book is printed on acid-free paper

HIGHLAND
REGIONAL
LIBRARY

1 800049839

1

Picture the Scenes

The Archway Players were holding their annual meeting. Things were not going well. Everyone seemed to be argumentative and no resolutions were even proposed, let alone agreed. It seemed the main problem was the next production. It would be just before Christmas and, for most of the group, pantomime was the obvious choice.

'Not a load of stupid people disagreeing with each other. 'Oh, no, he isn't'; 'Oh, yes, he is'. I can't bear it,' a rather forceful lady announced.

'I was thinking that we don't have to follow that sort of routine. Fairy stories are rather good and we could do a serious one. A proper love story,' the chairman said.

'How on earth would that work?' one

of the men asked. 'And where would we get a script from?'

'Write it ourselves if necessary. There's plenty of time before it needs to be ready. I'm sure it wouldn't be impossible. There are a couple of people out of work at the moment and a number of housewives who might help. How about it?'

'I love the idea,' Marie agreed. 'I think it could work well and I'd certainly be willing to help. I can type and it wouldn't have to be all that long. Oh, how exciting!'

Mrs Probert, a large lady with firm opinions and little acting talent, was the next to speak.

'Of all the ludicrous ideas, this one takes the biscuit. Playwrights take years to write anything halfway decent. How on earth do you expect amateurs to write a presentable play in a few weeks?'

It was the chairman's turn to speak next.

'Well, Marie has already volunteered

to type it. Who else would help?'

'I might be able to help. I'm not saying I could write it or anything, but I could certainly lend a hand.' This was Sally, a somewhat shy lady who thought she might come out of herself a bit if she was involved.

Adam, a young man who was almost guaranteed to take the main part, spoke next.

'I don't have much spare time, but I love this idea. Count me in. And I think my fiancée will help, too. She couldn't be here tonight unfortunately, as she's working.'

'It looks as if we're getting a team together. So are we all agreed? We will try to perform a non-traditional panto-mime based on one of the fairy stories.'

Two more people volunteered to join the writing party, with Mrs Probert still fuming and saying she wanted nothing more to do with the whole affair.

'In fact, I may decide to withdraw from the company.' She waited, expect-ing a flood of protests at her suggestion, but none came. She was furious and collected her handbag and notebook and left the room.

'Good riddance.' Marie grimaced. 'She drives me bonkers that one. But I bet she's back at the next meeting.'

There was a murmur of agreement from several of the other members.

The sub-committee was formed. It consisted of Adam, Marie, Sally, Jack — a retired salesman — and Adam's girlfriend, Gwen, even if she didn't know it yet.

'Who is going to be in charge?' Adam asked. 'I really don't want to be in charge in case there are any meetings I can't make.'

'If I'm doing the typing, I suppose it had better be me. If you all agree, of course,' Marie offered.

'Thanks, Marie. I'm happy with that. Any objections?'

There were none.

The next half hour was spent working out their strategy. They agreed on 'Cinderella' as the basis of the plot.

'We mustn't make it too unpleasant as there are bound to be children in the audience. She could just be worked too hard and left out of all family events,' Adam suggested.

The ugly sisters were the two older children of the master of the house and they liked to tease Cinders and make her do things they didn't want to do. She rarely complained.

'What about the 'going to the ball' scene?' Marie asked. 'We have to put that in somehow.'

'I think we should stop planning now,' Jack told them. 'Let's all go home and think about it. We know what the basic plot is and I'm sure we can all add various bits to it. Where are we going to meet? And when?'

Marie volunteered to let people come to her house.

'It's not very big, but I'm sure five or six of us can fit round the table. I must say, I'm really looking forward to getting started. How about we meet tomorrow evening? We can then all decide on different jobs to do.'

Soon everyone had agreed, including Adam who hadn't been too sure at the start. He had the task of letting his fiancée know she had been volunteered to help and wasn't sure if she would be free.

When he arrived home, he called Gwen.

'How are you? Had a good drama meeting?' she asked.

'Very good.'

'I'm glad. Sorry I wasn't there. So, what happened? What's the next production going to be?'

'We've decided on a non-traditional pantomime. We're going to tell the 'Cinderella' story in a straight way. You know, sort of modernised and brought up to date.'

'And where is the script coming from?'

'This is the point. I've said you and I will join a sub-committee to write it. There will be five of us working on it and Marie has volunteered to type it.

Can you make it to a meeting tomorrow evening?'

'Wow, that is ambitious. Are we actually capable of writing our own script?' Gwen asked.

'Of course we are. I'm actually quite excited at the thought of it all. I really hope you'll join in.' He paused and waited for her to say something. 'Well?'

'OK — but I'm not sure how much use I'll be.'

'You'll be great. We're meeting at Marie's house tomorrow at seven. Come here straight from work and I'll cook us something,' Adam said.

'That sounds fine. OK, I'll come with you tomorrow night. It might be interesting and possibly even fun.'

'Sleep well, love. Night.'

'Night.'

Adam gave a smile as he put the phone down. Gwen lived on the other side of town with her father and felt responsible for him. She was a health care worker and sometimes had to work an evening shift, as she had this evening.

7

He went and stood outside his flat and looked over the ocean. It would soon be too cold to go outside without a coat, but he adored Cornwall and all it had to offer.

He lived on the edge of a small town with a flourishing community spirit and had been a member of the Archway Players since he'd been a teenager.

Being a relatively young man, he was always very welcome in such a group who were always short of males to play a part in the various productions.

He saw himself in the role of Prince Charming, with Gwen playing Cinderella in this particular offering.

* * *

Just before seven o'clock the next evening, the pair walked round to Marie's house. It was in a row with a bright red front door. They knocked and were let in by Marie's husband, Dave.

'Come in. You're the first. Marie's

just saying goodnight to the kids. Won't be a minute. You're Adam, aren't you? So you must be Gwen.'

Gwen nodded.

Dave ushered them through to the kitchen.

'Make yourselves at home. I'll go and find Marie. I think this is going to take up a lot of her time, but then she's at home all day when the kids are at school.'

'How old are they?' Gwen wanted to know.

'Five and seven. Two girls and they are total imps. Keep us all busy, they do. I'll go and get Marie,' he repeated.

When he was upstairs, the doorbell rang again. Adam went to answer it. It was Jack and Sally who had met outside.

'Come on in. I've taken over as doorman. I think we're all here now. Marie's putting the children to bed.'

They all went into the kitchen and sat down at the table. Sally spoke first.

'I've had so many ideas and have

been buzzing all day. I think we need to make it all modern. They go to a disco rather than a ball.'

'Do people still go to discos?' Gwen asked with a smile.

'Oh, I don't know. Well, I suppose it could be a ball of some sort. Cindy, that's the girl's name, isn't allowed to go, but she goes anyway and watches through the window. Oh, there's all sorts of things we can do. And we don't have to have a prince. That's not really up to date, is it?'

'It looks as if you've given it a lot of thought,' Adam said. 'Well done.'

Marie entered the room, full of apologies.

'I am sorry. Typical kids. They knew I was going to be busy this evening and really played up. Dave is with them reading the umpteenth story. Now, would you like tea or coffee? Or I've got a bottle of wine.'

'That sounds wonderful. I'll bring some next time,' Jack offered.

'Right. I'll get us some glasses and

then we can get going. I must say, I'm rather excited.'

'Me, too. I was just saying I've had lots of ideas.' Sally seemed to have forgotten her shyness and was bubbling with excitement.

Soon, they all sat with a glass of wine in front of them and notepads at the ready.

'Now, then,' Jack began. 'I feel it might be easier if we think of various people in our group who can take particular roles. It might be easier to write for specific people, if you know what I mean. Adam will undoubtedly be the prince character, whatever he is in this production. What about Cindy?'

'I'd like to propose Gwen,' Adam said. 'Unless you think there's someone better, of course. Sorry, that sounds a bit selfish of me.'

'We can leave that one for now. You may be right. Adam is just about the only member we have who could play the male lead,' Jack said.

Adam blushed and acknowledged the compliment.

'I don't expect to play the male lead all the time, you know. If anyone else wants to take over, feel free.'

'I think perhaps I'll rival you.' Jack made them all laugh. 'A seventy-year-old dashing hero . . . Yes, I can just see it!'

'No, you're set for the father, Baron Hardup, as in the original story. You've fallen on hard times and try to watch every penny, but your two daughters want to spend everything that they possibly can. Some lovely arguments can ensue as they spend money online!' Marie looked triumphant as she spoke.

They began to map out the various scenes and put them together to make acts. By nine-thirty, they had the bare bones all planned. Characters were listed and even the sets were planned. They all agreed it must be kept simple as money was going to be tight and their talents were limited.

'Can we meet again soon?' Marie

asked. 'We need to make a start on the script while the enthusiasm is still with us. I'm free all week.'

'How about tomorrow? If we don't go on too late, I can do it.' Sally had really come out of herself and made several good suggestions. She had even offered to come and help Marie with the typing during the day, while the children were at school.

'Tomorrow's OK with me. How about you, Gwen?'

'Yes, I should be able to make it.'

'I am constantly free, or perhaps inexpensive,' Jack announced pompously, making them laugh again.

'Tomorrow it is, then. We'll make a start on the dialogue and I'll type up what we've got so far with copies for everyone,' Marie announced.

'Keep a note of what you're spending on paper. It's going to cost you quite a lot by the time we're finished,' Jack said.

'And ink cartridges as well. They don't come cheap. In fact, I can probably get us some from work. What sort of printer do you have?'

Adam and Marie went off to look, while Gwen washed the glasses and Sally dried them. The others returned and they all said their goodnights.

'I thought that all went very well, didn't you?' Gwen said in the car on their way back to Adam's flat.

'Very good. I just hope the dialogue proves fairly easy to write as well. I did wonder if we should all ad-lib. You know, like they do in some of those arty films.'

'I don't see how that would work. No, I think you've got to have proper lines and everyone needs to learn them.'

'We'll see. Maybe it will all work out.' Gwen nodded.

'It had better. We shall be in trouble if it doesn't!'

2

The Plot Thickens . . .

Gradually, the script was being put together by the committee. There were a few disagreements over some lines, but on the whole it was coming together well.

They had been set a deadline of three weeks after the original meeting when the first draft was to be completed.

The day before the deadline meeting, Marie printed a couple of copies of the entire script and brought it along to the meeting.

The room was full and everyone very keen to see what the sub-committee had come up with. Adam had been volunteered to read some of the scenes to the rest of group once Jack had outlined the plot and various acts.

He also told them how the scenery

would work, with a small section of the stage lit by spotlights as they were featured with the actions. They all thought this was a splendid idea.

'There are still some modifications to be made to the script so there aren't copies for anyone except Adam and the chairman, who will be directing the show.'

'Thank you, sir. I shall look forward to reading it. Most gratifying.' Mr Paul Mabberly accepted his copy graciously.

Adam began to read. They had picked on several scenes for him to read, hoping to give them all a taste of the whole thing. There were still a few holes waiting to be filled, but there was enough for everyone to get a picture of what would happen. He began to read. He was very good at producing different characters and they were all most impressed.

His voice rose when he was playing the two daughters and fell into a deep bass when he was their father. Jack sat with a smile on his face, imagining himself in the part. When Adam had finished, there was a round of applause.

'That was marvellous. I really enjoyed it. Thank you very much. I'm sure you will all agree with me that we are fortunate to have so talented an actor in our midst,' Paul said.

'Here, here,' was the general response, as they all applauded.

'Well, thank you. I think with a couple more sessions of working, we shall soon have the whole thing ready. I was wondering about paying for paper and ink. We can't expect Marie to pay for it all. It will be quite a package to print off for everyone,' Paul added.

'Yes, indeed,' Alexander Metcalfe, the treasurer, said. 'We usually have to pay fees for a script we use and the copies for individuals. It can come from that budget. Well done to all of you. You are an excellent sub-committee.'

'I wonder if we're not selling ourselves short,' Mrs Probert put in. 'It's all very amateurish, isn't it? I mean, none of us are playwrights. I really feel very strongly that we should be looking at a good Agatha Christie or some comedy. Our audience expects it from us.'

'Well, they'll get a change then, won't they?' Marie told her. She was furious with the woman who always seemed to sit back and criticise and never did anything to help.

'Really. I don't know what the young people of today are thinking about. You need to apologise for your show of bad manners.'

'Apologise? Me? Not on your . . . '

'That's enough now.' Paul Mabberly stepped in to avoid an open row. 'I think we should call it a day. Let's all go through to the bar and I'll treat all of you on the sub-committee to a drink.'

'Thanks. A very good idea,' Adam agreed.

'Honestly, that woman . . . she's enough to drive anyone to drink,' Marie murmured to Adam. 'It's not as if she ever does anything to help, is it? Always

18

ready to find fault and never willing to do anything. Anyway, let's forget about her. You do read very well, you know. We're lucky to have you available to play the lead. It's a pity you can't play all the parts, if your reading was anything to go by.'

Adam smiled.

'You're very kind. I did enjoy it, actually. Maybe I'm just a frustrated actor at heart.'

The evening soon drew to a close. They agreed to one more meeting to tidy up the script and then the big print-off could begin. They agreed on a copy for each member of the cast plus a couple of extras for the director and eventually the prompt. They could always print off more if necessary.

'Are you sure you can do them all, Marie?' Adam asked her.

'I should think so. We could do with folders for them, don't you think? They'll get very tatty by the time we're ready to perform.'

'I'll get some for us. I'm sure I can

buy them through work. It shouldn't be a problem.'

By the time they were all printed, Marie announced she never wanted to see a computer again.

★ ★ ★

The next meeting was to be the casting meeting. Everyone was equal and there were no prejudices about the parts. Adam was presuming he'd get the male lead and Gwen perhaps the main female part. Apart from his hopes, he was ready to accept whatever came along.

'Right,' Paul announced, who had been elected to be the director, as usual, 'who would like to read what?'

'Erm . . . I'd like to . . . to read for Cindy,' a young girl said.

She was a fairly new member of the group and was being encouraged by Geoffrey, her father, who pushed her forward and prompted her. He nodded approvingly.

'And I see myself as the father,' Jack announced. He knew there were some good lines in there and he was ready to make the most of them.

'How about the two sisters?' Paul asked. 'Marie and Sally? How about you try for them?'

The two women giggled and agreed. 'Could be fun. OK.'

Soon all the parts were allocated, leaving Gwen without anything and Adam reluctant to take part without her. The young girl read reasonably well and was given the part of Cindy. She could look quite pathetic and might play the part quite well.

★ ★ ★

Rehearsals got underway, twice a week. They were all getting used to their parts. Adam wasn't at all happy about Cindy. Contrary to expectations, she put in no expression to the part and he despaired of it ever coming together.

It was all too soon the middle of November. Nobody knew their words and everyone was still clutching their scripts for every scene.

'Come on, people. It really is time you put some effort into learning your lines.' Paul was furious with them. 'You forget what you were told last week and have to be told again. It really isn't good enough. Adam, do you think Gwen would come in and prompt? I want you all to try to manage without your script next week. It really is getting critical.'

'I'll ask Gwen, but I'm not sure she'll be willing,' Adam admitted. 'She was very disappointed not to get a part, you realise. She just felt left out.'

'I'm sorry about that. I suppose it always happens to someone. See what she says anyhow. If she really doesn't want to do it there will be someone who does, I'm sure.'

It was all very well for him to make this suggestion. Gwen had been very put out by not being a part of this production and he'd had to put up with her bad mood.

They had missed several chances to see each other because of his rehearsals and he couldn't see her wanting to do any favours for Paul. He rather dreaded having to ask her. On the other hand, it would mean she would be there with him.

After the rehearsal, he decided to call her.

'Hello, you,' he said cheerfully.

'Oh, hello.' She didn't sound too happy to hear from him.

'How are you?'

'Fine.'

'Can we meet tomorrow?'

'Oh, an evening off. No rehearsal? Wow, that will make a change.'

'I'm sorry, love. You know how it is as the production date approaches.'

'I remember it well. Best of luck to you. Is there anything else? Only I'm tired and want to go to bed.'

'Tomorrow?' He decided it was not the right time to ask her now, so he would wait till tomorrow and ask her face to face.

'I'm not sure. I might be going out with some of the girls from work, you know.'

'Oh. Only I haven't seen you for ages. Well, for three nights anyway.'

'And whose fault is that? That wretched drama group.'

'I'm sorry. Perhaps you could give me a ring tomorrow if you are free.'

'OK. Night.'

'Night, love.'

Gwen ended the call and Adam sat looking at his own mobile in disbelief. He'd had no idea she felt so strongly about his involvement with the group.

He put on his computer and decided to send her some flowers. A couple of clicks and they would be sent the next day.

He went to bed and settled down with his script to learn. He was asleep before he reached the end of the first page.

3

Bad News

The next morning, Adam pondered over whether to ring Gwen or not. He finally decided to call her at lunchtime.

'How about this evening, Gwen? Are you free or not? I thought we could maybe go out for a meal or I could cook something at home. You can choose.'

She hesitated before she spoke.

'OK, let's go out for a pub meal. Anything else? Only I'm just about to start with a new patient.'

'Er . . . no. Nothing else.'

'Right. See you at seven.' And she rang off. No goodbye or loving message.

He hoped the flowers had been delivered and that might melt the ice a little. She hadn't mentioned them, but then perhaps she had left home before they were delivered.

He didn't like this chilly atmosphere between them. He was actually beginning to think of proposing to her, but lately it had seemed less of a good plan. It seemed a long day to him and he looked forward to the evening, hoping things would be sorted out between them.

Gwen arrived promptly at seven. She greeted him with a kiss and an apology.

'Sorry if I've been a bit off lately. We've had a few problems at work. Jenny's leaving and it's been difficult to fit in all her clients with the rest of us. And you've been so involved with your wretched play, I've hardly seen you.'

'I know and I'm sorry. But that could all end. Paul has asked me to ask you — even beg you — to come and act as prompt. We desperately need you. We have to manage without the scripts at the next rehearsal and everyone is very nervous about it. What do you think? At least we'd be doing the same thing, wouldn't we?'

'I don't know . . . ' Gwen mused. 'It's a pretty boring life being a prompt.'

'I know. I wasn't sure if it was a good idea to ask you. What do you think?'

'I suppose so. Yes, OK, I'll do it.'

'Brilliant. We'll all be so grateful. Paul's been trying to do it as well as directing, but it isn't really working. That's excellent.'

'Did you send some flowers to the house today?' Gwen asked.

'Well, yes. I felt we were having a few problems and wanted to show you I really do love you. Why do you ask?'

'There was no signature or message and we didn't know. Dad thought some-one actually fancied him.' She laughed.

'Oh, dear. It's the price of doing these things much too late in the evening. Sorry. They really were for you, of course.'

'Oh, Adam. You really are a dear. Thank you so much. I'll tell Dad later. I'll leave him to his delusions for now.'

A couple of days later, Gwen was sitting to one side of the stage clutching her copy of the script. She was appalled by how few of the group actually knew their lines. One chap started on a speech about three pages further on which would have led to complete confusion.

'No, no, no!' she called out loudly, 'You're leaping further ahead and missing out a lot of speeches and action. I'm sorry,' she said to the director, 'but it's vital to the plot.'

'I quite agree. Geoffrey, you really do need to learn your lines.'

'Oh, really. Don't make such a fuss. I make it all fit in beautifully. It's what I do. That's why I always get good reviews. I'm not having some silly young girl telling me how to act.' He flounced off the stage and went into the bar.

'I'm sorry,' Gwen apologised to the group.

'Don't mention it. He never appreciates the effect he has on the rest of us. Good for you for pointing it out.' This was one of the other older actors who was very experienced in their plays.

'Right,' Paul called out, 'we'll have the scene with Cindy and the ugly sisters, where Cindy is chiding them for all their online shopping.'

Gwen listened to the three girls. The so-called ugly sisters were really comedy characters and had some excellent lines. She found herself smiling as she was reading the carefully crafted lines.

Cindy, she decided, was adequate, but really didn't make much of her role. Gwen looked at Paul to see what he was thinking but he remained impassive.

Who was the young girl anyway? Gwen would ask Adam later.

The evening wore on and Gwen's impatience grew with every fluff in the lines. Still, she convinced herself, this was the first time many of them were working without the comfort of scripts in their hands. Whatever she thought of their performances, it wasn't up to her to comment.

'Well done, love,' Adam said afterwards.

'You were very good, Adam,' Gwen told him.

'Thank you.' Adam smiled. 'What do you think of Cindy?'

'Do I have to be honest?'

'Oh, dear. That good, eh? She's Geoffrey's daughter. I think Paul felt he should give her a go, for her father's sake.'

'I did wonder.'

'It's such a pity you're not doing the role,' Adam said. 'I know when we wrote it, I had you in mind for the part. Still, hopefully she'll come good in the end.'

'Hmm. She's completely dead in the part at the moment.'

They suddenly became aware of someone standing behind them. It was Margaret, Geoffrey's wife. She was clearly furious.

'How dare you talk like that about

my daughter? She has taken this role as her first performance. I think she's doing extremely well, whatever you say. I shall complain to Paul about you both. You're both being so unfair to poor Crystal.' She stalked away and went in search of Paul to make her complaint.

'Oh, it serves her right for listening into other people's conversations.' Gwen was quite disturbed.

'Don't worry about it. I bet Paul agrees completely. He doesn't know how to deal with it. Frankly, I think he's scared of Geoffrey.'

'Oh, yes, I'd forgotten about that particular fracas. Perhaps I'd better resign as prompt right now.'

Adam shook his head.

'Don't even go there. You've done nothing wrong. And as for Geoffrey, well, he deserved everything you said. So, no more worries, OK?'

'I suppose you're right.'

★ ★ ★

The next morning, Adam received a phone call from Paul. It was bad news.

'It looks as though we've lost Cindy — Crystal, I mean. She was attacked last night and is now in hospital, fighting for her very life, according to Geoffrey. I really don't see how we can go on. I'm phoning round to let everyone know.'

'Goodness me! Do they know who did it? How badly is she injured?'

'Apparently she's critical. A broken leg amongst other things, but it's her head injuries they're mostly concerned about.'

'That's awful. Poor girl.'

Adam's mind raced on to thoughts about the play. Would anyone want to continue with it — or had this put the skids under it? After all the work they'd put into it, writing it, casting and learning lines . . .

Then he immediately felt guilty for thinking about the play when the poor girl's life was hanging in the balance.

4

Mad Proposal

Adam rang Gwen to tell her the news.

'Oh my goodness, how awful!' Gwen exclaimed. 'She will recover, though, won't she? I can't imagine who would do anything like that to her. She's so quiet and inoffensive.'

'I know. I don't think they know yet how it happened. Sounds to me as though she was run over rather than beaten up. That's just me speculating, though. Whatever caused it, it's most unpleasant.'

'What do you think will happen to the play?' Gwen asked. 'Will they abandon it now?'

'I don't know. I doubt Geoffrey will want to continue. I'd think there may be a meeting to discuss what to do.'

'Well, keep me posted and I'll see you there. I have to get back to work now.'

* * *

It was fortunate that Paul was retired. He seemed to have spent more or less the whole day on the phone, getting opinions and speaking to the cast members. He finally agreed to hold an emergency meeting that evening to allow everyone to have their say and take a vote on whether to continue with the play or not.

'My thanks to those of you who have managed to attend. We now have to decide whether or not we're going to carry on with this play. I must say, it would be a pity to lose out on all the work that has been done.'

'How is Cindy — I mean Crystal?' someone asked.

'She's making progress, but certainly won't be able to take her part. No, we shall have to re-cast if we are to go ahead. What do we all think?' There was sudden buzz of conversation round the room.

'I say go ahead with it.' Sally spoke up. 'Gwen can play Cindy and I'm sure she'll do a good job of it.'

Several of the others made murmurings of agreement.

'I think you should abandon it. There are so many flaws in the play and it will be an embarrassment to us all. This is surely a sign we should abandon the whole thing.' Mrs Probert made her usual comments but was shouted down.

'Assuming no-one else agrees with Mrs Probert, let's consider what lies ahead,' Paul said. 'Time is very short. We might be asking a bit much of Gwen to learn it in such a short time. What do you think?'

'Don't forget I helped write the piece. I'm sure I could do it, if you feel sufficiently confident in me.' Gwen blushed as she was speaking. Adam reached over and grabbed her hand encouragingly.

'So, that's settled. I'm not sure about

Geoffrey. Has anyone spoken to him?'

'I spoke to him later this morning after I heard of the accident,' Marie said. 'He was obviously very concerned about his daughter and very angry that anyone could have done this. He didn't mention the play, of course.'

'Well, he doesn't have a huge part so we can leave that for the time being. Someone can stand in for him. Well, Gwen, congratulations and I hope you really can learn your lines in time. I'll have to find someone else to prompt. Everyone except Gwen, learn your lines and be prepared to do it completely without your scripts. I'll see you all tomorrow evening.'

* * *

The following evening, Adam and Gwen met up at the hall. It was part of a large industrial organisation and housed their social club, as well as providing the group with a venue for their plays. They all appreciated being allowed to use the hall for rehearsals as well as for the performances.

When they arrived, it was to hear Mrs Probert sounding off at anyone who would listen.

'I always knew this was a ridiculous idea. Surely this proves it. Poor little Crystal, lying there in her bed of sickness and pain. I reckon we all know who we think did this. Whose girlfriend in now taking over Crystal's role? Stands to reason.' She had her back to the door and was unaware of Adam's presence in the room.

Adam went white with anger. How dare she accuse him, for obviously he was the person she was insinuating was guilty.

He took a deep breath to control himself and then spoke.

'Mrs Probert, I don't know where you got the outrageous idea I could have done such a thing — injured Cindy . . . Crystal, I mean.'

'I have my sources.'

'Oh, really? I think I'm entitled to

know, don't you?'

'Adam, you know it wasn't you. Don't let her think she's won.' Gwen was becoming very anxious.

'I want to know who told her it was me. My name is being blackened by someone and I need to know who. So, Mrs Probert, who was it?' Adam moved closer to her and looked very threatening.

'Get away from me! See how aggressive he is?' she burbled to anyone who would listen. 'He's going to attack me like he attacked Crystal.'

Adam could stand it no longer.

'You really are pathetic. I don't know why you even show your face here. I did not attack Crystal and certainly wouldn't touch you with a barge pole. Why don't you go home and leave us to our rehearsal? And don't you dare spread any more vicious rumours about me or I'll be speaking to my solicitor.'

'And there speaks a guilty man,' she retorted as she left the room.

'I am not guilty,' Adam said firmly.

'You can't believe that I am. I was willing to make the best of Crystal playing Cindy, but I think we all have to admit she wasn't the best choice.' He was speaking to a couple of the cast who had been listening in sympathy for him during Mrs Probert's tirade. 'That woman's bonkers. What does she do for the group? I've yet to see her lift a finger to do anything. She always swans around when we're actually doing a performance and makes people think she's vital to it all. I think she should be kicked out.'

There was a murmur of agreement from several of the others.

Paul arrived and sensed a conflict.

'What's going on?'

'That wretched Probert woman spreading her evil. She actually accused Adam of injuring Crystal so I could have her part. Honestly. I could hardly credit the woman's gall,' Gwen replied.

'I feel awful,' she continued. 'Can we change the subject, please? I've been working hard all day learning my lines. I want to see how much I can remember.'

Adam took her hand and gave it a squeeze and she smiled at him.

Paul was ready to begin.

'Good idea, people. Let's go through to the hall and make a start. From the beginning, please.'

Cindy and her sisters were on first and Adam gave Gwen's hand another squeeze as she climbed up to the stage.

'Go get 'em, love,' he whispered.

She grinned.

'I'll do my best.'

Paul was delighted with her progress and told her so. The rest of the cast were impressed with her performance and agreed between themselves that she was much better than Crystal had been.

'Let's make a start on the next scene. Can someone prompt, please? No scripts anywhere except for Gwen. She can have hers if she needs it, though from what I've seen so far, she doesn't need much prompting. Well done, lass. Great job.'

Halfway through the next scene, Geoffrey came into the hall.

'Hello, everyone,' he said loudly, interrupting the action. 'I thought you'd like to know the latest news on Crystal. She is much better. She does have a broken leg but in a few days she will be more mobile. I suspect she will want to come back to take her part. Nobody will mind if she has a cast on her leg, will they? We might have to change the scenario for the ball scene, but I'm sure she'll cope.'

He looked around the group, who were stunned into silence.

'Well, good news, don't you think? She can continue to learn her lines and perhaps even hold a rehearsal at home. Now, where are we at with tonight's shenanigans? Have I missed my bit or do I come in soon?'

Nobody quite knew what to say. They certainly didn't want Crystal back in the role of Cindy, and presumably with

41

a cast on her leg, she shouldn't even attempt it. They looked at Paul to say something. He took a deep breath and finally spoke.

'I'm sure we're all delighted Crystal hasn't sustained more damage. Please pass on our good wishes to her. The thing is, we've re-cast her role and Gwen has worked hard to learn the lines and is doing really well.'

'What? You mean Gwen is going to play Crystal's part?' Geoffrey cried. 'That's hardly fair, is it? My daughter's worked very hard to learn the part and was relying on being able to carry on with it. She will be devastated if she has to lose it. It's the main reason she's making such progress, to get back here with all of us.'

'We didn't know that,' Paul told him. 'We needed to continue with rehearsals and this seemed the best solution. Please pass on our apologies to Crystal. Next time, perhaps.'

Geoffrey looked shattered at the news.

'Geoffrey, my dear chap,' Paul said gently, 'we were all devastated to hear of Crystal's accident . . . '

'Oh, it was no accident. She was beaten up by someone who wanted to replace her in this role. I was talking to Mrs Probert and she voiced her suspicions to me.'

He glanced furiously at Adam and looked as if he was about to sound off, but someone went to him and began to chat quietly to calm him down.

The cast resumed the play. Gwen was a great success and they all congratulated her on the amount she had learned.

'I think you did tremendously,' Adam told her. 'You're a natural for the part.'

'That's not what Geoffrey thinks. He was practically spitting fire at me. And he really does seem to think you were responsible for dear Crystal's so-called accident.'

'I'm getting sick of being under suspicion. As if I'd do anything like that, especially to get you a part in some silly play.

'Let's go home,' he went on. 'I want to get away from this toxic atmosphere. I think Geoffrey has just gone into the bar and I really don't want to hear more of his insinuations.'

'Suits me. Goodnight, everyone,' Gwen called out.

'Bye, you two. Good show, Gwen. Keep it up.'

Hand in hand, they walked out and back to Adam's flat. They discussed the evening and asked each other who could really have injured Crystal. They both agreed they had no idea what sort of person she was or who her friends were. She always seemed to be so protected by Geoffrey.

'Sally said she'd heard Crystal was hanging round with that crowd of druggies from the estate at one point,' Gwen told him.

'Really? I wouldn't have thought Geoffrey would like that.'

'Oh, he didn't. He banned her from

ever seeing them again apparently. But I think she was still seeing that Rocky character. I'm sure I saw her with him one night after we'd been to the pub.'

'I wouldn't have thought he was at all her type,' Adam pointed out.

'I think she was rebelling against her father. He is such a snob. Maybe she is still seeing him without letting on.'

'Come on. Let's get back to the flat. I'm freezing. Besides, there's an idea I've had that I want to talk about.'

'And what's that?'

'Wait till we get back to my place. Curb your curiosity.'

The pair walked quickly back to his flat. He turned on the gas fire and went into the kitchen and put the kettle on.

Gwen sat down in front of the growing heat and held out her hands to the warmth. The weather was certainly turning much colder.

Here in Cornwall they didn't often get snow, but she felt it was certainly getting cold enough for it now.

Adam came back with two steaming mugs of coffee.

'There you are. Get that inside you. You'll soon warm up.'

'Come on, then,' Gwen urged. 'What did you want to tell me.'

'You know the wedding scene at the end of the play?'

'Of course I do.'

'And then there's a sort of reception.'

'Yes.' Gwen was becoming impatient.

'Well, suppose we got married earlier in the day? It could be our reception for real. We could make an announcement to the audience when everyone's getting their bouquets and so on.' Adam began to look nervous. 'How about it? The after-show party could be a further bit of our reception.'

Gwen looked shocked.

'I think you're completely bonkers!' She laughed. 'How on earth could we arrange all that? Goodness me. How am I expected to organise a wedding in that short space of time?'

'I thought you'd leap at the chance.

46

There's no-one else to consider. Well, apart from your father, but he'd be willing to go with it surely?'

'What about friends, though?' She shook her head. 'No, it's quite impossible. They'd never forgive me. And what would I wear?'

'Oh. I suppose you would want a long white frothy dress and all the bits and pieces that go with it. Sorry, just forget it. I wasn't thinking.'

Gwen frowned.

'Of course I wouldn't. I'd never want to look like a meringue, and I certainly don't want a big affair. The registry office is what I was thinking of. But do you really want to do it like this?'

'I wouldn't have suggested it if I didn't. I just thought it seemed like such a good idea.'

'Maybe it isn't such a bad one. Let me think about it. I must get home now or Dad will think I'm missing. And I've got an early start tomorrow.'

'Promise me you will think about it?' Adam asked.

'I will. The Saturday morning, you think? At the registry office?'

'Yes. Your dad will keep it a secret, won't he?'

'Yes, I'm sure he would. Let me give some thought to it, as I say. I'm just not sure if it's practical. I'd better go now. See you soon.'

Adam watched her as she got into her car and drove away.

'Fingers crossed,' he whispered as her tail lights disappeared.

5

A Thief in the Night

The next day Adam called Gwen as he drove back home from the office.

'Hi, Gwen. Hope you get this message. Also, I hope that you're planning to come over this evening. Speak later.'

It was already very dark as he parked the car. As he got out there was a scuttle as someone hid behind another car.

He went over to look but the person had run away, leaped over the sea wall and disappeared.

Strange, he thought.

He gave a shrug and went into his flat. His phone was ringing as he entered the living-room so he rushed to answer it.

'Hi, Adam. Only me.' It was Gwen's

voice. 'I'm afraid I won't be over tonight as Dad's not well. Just a cold or something, but he needs me around. You know how man flu can be.

'About your wedding idea . . . I spoke about it to Dad — not that it did much good as he was too bogged down with his cold. He just said I should do what I wanted.'

'And what is that?'

'Well, assuming it will be a very small affair . . . OK. Let's do it.'

'Oh, Gwen, that's wonderful. I'm delighted. It won't matter to me about having a small wedding, but I hope you don't feel deprived. If we're having a party in the evening anyway, it'll be like a reception.'

'We must add stuff to the food, though. And perhaps provide a wedding cake. I think it could be really lovely,' Gwen said.

'I think it will be marvellous. Oh, you've made my day. I want to hug you! I suppose I couldn't come over to see you, could I?'

'I'm not sure it would be a good idea,' she replied. 'Dad's asleep in the living-room. I've just left him there and I'm phoning from the kitchen.'

'I can be very quiet. Promise.'

'Well . . . '

'I'm on my way.'

Adam left the house, only just remembering to lock his door. He almost ran round to the car park then stopped dead. He was sure he had parked in his usual place, but it was empty. There was no sign of any car there, or anywhere else.

He walked a little way along the road, peering through the darkness, but he couldn't see a thing. It was also beginning to rain. There was nothing he could do so he went back into the flat and picked up the phone to call Gwen.

'Gwen, my car's been stolen!' he cried. 'I'm about to phone the police but thought I'd better let you know. At least I won't be guilty of waking your dad.'

'Oh, that's awful. Who could have taken it?'

'No idea. There was someone hanging around when I got home but he ran off and jumped over the sea wall. He must have come back. I'd better go now and phone the police.'

'OK. Good luck.'

Adam called the police and told them his story.

'I've no idea who the person was that I saw. Not that I really saw him clearly. He ran away when he saw me. I'm assuming it was a him and not a her.'

'Someone will call round later this evening to take the details,' the officer told him. 'Bad business. It's a pretty dark night so difficult to see anything. Right you are, sir. See you later.'

Adam hung up and sat cursing the person who had pinched his car. His former elation at Gwen's words had now disappeared as he contemplated the problems that lay ahead.

How would he get to work in the morning? And home again? Then there was the weekend ahead with all they had to do if their plans were going to work.

He picked up his phone again and called Gwen. He explained the police would be calling and voiced his concerns about his lack of transport for getting to work the following day.

'I can come and take you,' Gwen offered, 'and possibly collect you, too.'

'I don't want to put you to all that trouble.'

'Don't worry. I can easily fit it all in. I don't start till later tomorrow and only have a short shift. Dad will be all right by then.'

Adam was relieved.

'Well, thanks. I'm grateful. I just hope the police can find it. It's nothing very special, my car. I'm sure it must be someone being spiteful or trying to get at me for some unknown reason.'

'Let me know if there's anything else I can do.'

'Thanks. About the wedding . . . did you really mean it?'

'Of course. I've told Dad, of course, but we'll need someone to be a witness.'

'Leave it till nearer the time. I love you. You're being so great about it all.'

'I might even wear my dress from the play. Who knows!' Gwen laughed.

'I thought it was bad luck for me to see the dress before the wedding?'

'You may be right. I'll see. Better go. I can hear Dad moving around.'

'OK. Night, love. I expect the police will be here soon,' Adam replied. 'I'll see you in the morning around eight-thirty.'

'No problem. Night.' Gwen hung up and he gave a wry smile. Then he gave a small whoop of pleasure.

Gwen had agreed to his crazy plan to get married in just a few weeks. He would have to go to the registry office and book it. Hopefully they wouldn't be too busy at this time of year. Two weeks later it would be Christmas and then it would probably be impossible.

He heard someone knock at his door

and he opened it to find a policeman standing there.

Adam repeated his story to the constable, who made a few notes and nodded several times.

'Right, we'll keep a look out for it. There's been a spate of car thefts lately, though usually they go for a more special model. Sorry, I'm not being rude, but this is a bit out of the ordinary. It looks more like a personal thing rather than a theft. Is there anyone who may have a grudge or some other reason for taking it?'

Adam shook his head, thinking.

'I don't think so. I'm very involved in amateur dramatics. I haven't had time for much else lately. We're doing a production in a few weeks so rehearsals are filling up most of my spare time.'

The police officer raised his eyebrows.

'Any problems there for you? Someone who doesn't like what you're doing?'

Again Adam shook his head.

'No, I don't think so. They're a friendly bunch and we all get on very well — apart from one lady who is never satisfied, but she'd never steal a car in a million years.' He almost smiled at the thought of Mrs Probert doing anything worse than moan. Then he remembered her spiteful accusations.

'The only accident we've had was for someone who was playing the lead female role,' Adam continued. 'But she had to drop out and my fiancée took the role instead. Sorry, but there's no way she could have taken my car even if she could drive.'

'Who was that?'

'Crystal Parkinson. Her father is Geoffrey Parkinson. He's also in the play. Only a small part this time, but he has played much bigger parts, not particularly well, I may add. Sorry, I'm blabbing on and this is all a bit irrelevant.'

'Not at all, sir. Anything you can tell me might help. And is Crystal angry about losing her part?'

'I don't know. I haven't seen her. Her father wanted her to continue in the play. But with a plaster cast on her leg, she could hardly be Cinderella, could she?'

'Oh, so it's a panto, is it? I might take my little lad to see it.'

'It's not exactly a panto . . . We're just using the Cinderella story as a background. It's a sort of comedy,' Adam explained.

'Right. Well, I'd better get back to the station now. I'll put in a report about your car. Good evening, sir.'

Adam saw him out and looked around before he closed the door. Everything seemed quiet and nobody was around.

He wondered what to do next. It was too early to go to bed and there was nothing he wanted to watch on television.

He realised he hadn't eaten so he found some bread and cheese and made himself a sandwich. Things would change when he was living with Gwen.

They'd have to shop a lot more and have proper, regular meals.

He smiled at the thought. It was all going to be wonderful when they were married.

He began to think about how they would organise the wedding. In his mind, they would get married in the morning then go through the matinee performance as they usually did.

During the evening, when they came to the wedding scene, he would step forward and tell everyone they were married and invite the cast to celebrate after the show.

He thought he'd say they'd like everyone to attend, but realised it would make far too large a number with the entire audience. He smiled at the prospect.

★　★　★

After work the next day, Adam asked Gwen to drive round to the registry office where they were able to book a slot for the wedding. Unfortunately they were only able to book a slot slightly later than they would have chosen.

'It'll make it a bit tight before the matinee performance. Is that all right with you?' Adam asked Gwen.

'Of course it is. I won't have time to get nervous, will I?'

'You? Nervous? Never.'

They both laughed together then drove back to his flat.

'Shall we go out to eat?' Adam suggested. 'I don't have much in the fridge.'

'I really should go back to see Dad. He was staying at home today and will undoubtedly be feeling neglected. You can come, too, if you like,' Gwen offered. Adam nodded.

'Yes, please. Otherwise I'd probably just slump here feeling sorry for myself. I'll just give the police a call to see if they've got my car back. Is that OK with you?'

'Of course.' Gwen put her arms

around his neck as he made his call and kissed him.

He pushed her away with a smile.

'Hello? I'm calling to see if you've any news about my car that was stolen last night. My name is Adam Jerrold.'

'Ah. Mr Jerrold,' the officer told him. 'Yes, I was just about to phone you. We've found a burned-out car of a similar make to yours.'

'What? Burned out?' His mouth dropped open.

'I'm afraid so. There were no number plates, of course, and it's very badly burned so we can't even tell what colour it was. We don't know for sure it's yours.'

'Good heavens. Where is it?'

'In a deserted place inland a little way, where they're planning to build a new housing estate.'

'I know where you mean,' Adam told the officer. 'Shall I go and look at it? My girlfriend's here with me so she'll drive me over there.'

'Well, you could. I doubt it'll do

much good, though. As I say, it's very badly burned. You should get in touch with your insurance company and arrange to hire a car in the meantime. We'll let you know as soon as we can confirm if it is your car or not. Maybe we'll be able to find something to prove it.'

Once he had ended the call, Adam told Gwen everything the office had said and called his insurance company. They arranged for him to hire a car the next morning.

'Do you mind taking me to where they've found a car? It may or may not be mine,' Adam asked Gwen.

'Of course not. Then I'll go home to see how Dad is.'

They drove the few miles to the place the police had mentioned. It was a large open space surrounded by trees, with a narrow track leading into it.

'It's down there,' Adam told her, 'between the hedges. That's it.'

Two police cars were parked beside a burned-out wreck and three officers stood looking at it, apparently discussing whether or not it was Adam's.

Adam and Gwen got out of Gwen's car and went over to the policemen.

'I think it was silver,' one of the officers said. 'There's still a bit of paint under what's left of the bonnet. There's nothing at all left inside it.'

Adam nodded.

'Sounds like mine. The scoundrels. Why steal it and then burn it? It seems a vicious thing to do. Who on earth hates me so much?' Adam was visibly upset.

'Don't worry, sir. I suspect it may be someone with a complaint about society rather than anything more sinister.'

Adam shook his head.

'That's easy enough to say, officer. It's still my car that's ruined.'

⋆   ⋆   ⋆

Adam felt very depressed as Gwen drove him back to his flat. He thought hard about who could have done this dreadful act of vandalism, but could come up with nothing helpful. He wondered if it could be some of the youths from the local housing estate but he'd had little or no contact with anyone from there.

As they drew up outside the flat, he turned to Gwen.

'You'd better get back to your dad. I'll stay here.'

'What about food? You said you didn't have anything in.'

'I'll ferret around the freezer. There's bound to be something there.'

'I am sorry, love. Just when we were so happy about the wedding and everything.'

'At least that's something good we've done today,' Adam said miserably. 'You go now. I'll be all right.'

Gwen hesitated.

'I don't like leaving you when you're so fed up. Are you sure you'll be all right?' she told him.

'Of course I will be,' Adam assured

her. 'You go and see your dad. I'll see you tomorrow at the rehearsal.'

'What about getting to work in the morning?' Gwen asked. 'I could come and collect you but it will have to be early. My shift starts at seven-thirty.'

'I'll go and collect my insurance hire car. I'll be fine.'

Adam watched Gwen drive away and went back into his flat. There was no point in moping, so he picked up his script and checked his lines. He realising he knew most of his script and this cheered him.

Later, he phoned Gwen to see how she was feeling.

'I'm fine,' she told him when she answered. 'Dad seems to be over his cold and was pleased to hear we'd booked the registry office. Don't worry, I've sworn him to secrecy. Have you eaten anything yet?'

'Oh, I forgot.'

'Make sure you do eat something before you have your early night,' Gwen told him and Adam laughed.

'I will. Goodnight, Mrs Jerrold-to-be.'

'Oh, that sounds rather good. Gwendolyn Jerrold. I like it.'

6

Change of Plans

Adam walked round to the garage the next morning to collect his hire car. He explained the situation and told them he'd have to buy a new car soon.

The girl behind the counter looked very interested and asked if he'd be coming to them to buy it.

'It all depends on my insurance company.' Adam shrugged. 'As soon as they give me the go ahead, I'll start looking. Anyway, which car do I get for now?'

She gave Adam a set of keys, and once he'd signed the papers he went out to their yard and clicked the key to see which was his car. It was the same model his own car had been, so he felt quite pleased.

His day at work seemed to speed by,

much to his delight, and soon he was driving towards Gwen's home with the idea of collecting her and taking her for a meal before the rehearsal.

'I thought you'd be round,' Gwen said cheerfully. 'I've cooked us a meal so come on in. You can chat to Dad while I finish it off. How's the hire car by the way?'

'Similar to my old one.'

'That's good. Go on through.'

Adam went through to the lounge and sat down with Mr Harper.

'I'm delighted to hear the news, lad,' Gwen's dad told him with a smile. 'I know how much it means to Gwennie.'

Adam smiled at hearing her dad's name for her.

'It'll be good to see you both married,' her dad added.

'I hope it won't be too much of a shock to lose her. We'll be living in my flat to start with, but hopefully we'll get a house before too long.' Adam didn't notice Mr Harper's expression as he said this.

'I didn't know that was part of your plan,' Gwen's dad said. 'I always assumed you'd move in here. There's plenty of room and it's all furnished. And I wouldn't be looking for any rent from you. I don't need any more money and this place is paid for.'

'That's very generous of you. We haven't really discussed it yet. I just assumed we'd be living at my place.' Adam suddenly felt very uncomfortable, as this was certainly not what he wanted at all.

He wanted them to be independent and to live their own lives away from her father . . . not that he had anything against her father. They'd always got on very well.

Fortunately, Gwen came into the room at that point to announce the meal was ready.

Adam looked at her with a slightly quizzical smile. He hadn't actually asked her what she wanted and had merely assumed they'd live in his flat to start with. Perhaps he'd been a bit hasty in suggesting they got married so quickly.

'I've made a pie,' Gwen announced unnecessarily as she put it on the table.

'So I see,' her father said. 'You're nearly as good as your mum was. Keep practising, love, and we'll keep eating it.'

'Cheek!' Gwen exclaimed with a laugh.

Mr Harper offered to wash up so that Adam and Gwen could both relax for a while before going out to the rehearsal. They sat together in the lounge and Adam decided to raise the subject of where they were going to live.

'I don't know,' Gwen admitted. 'I suppose I thought it would be in your flat to start with. Why do you ask?'

'Your dad seems to think we'll be living here.'

Gwen nodded with a frown.

'I thought he might,' she said. 'Would that be a problem for you?'

'Well, yes. I'd always thought of us living in my flat and being able to do whatever we wanted, when we wanted.'

Gwen gave a giggle.

'I can see why you don't really want to live here. Oh dear, this raises a lot of problems, doesn't it? I knew he'd miss us, but we'd always pop in to see him and invite him round to the flat. He's not bad at looking after himself, but he does rely on me a lot of the time.'

'It's a pity he can't find another woman,' Adam said. 'Sorry, I didn't mean that unkindly.'

'No, you're right.' Gwen nodded. 'He's never bothered because I've always been here. Perhaps it is time he started socialising again.'

'Perhaps he could come and join the drama group,' Adam said with a grin.

'What's this?' Gwen's dad asked as he came into the room again. 'Me join the drama group? One person being an actor is quite enough for this family, thank you very much. Now, can I get you a coffee?'

'No, thanks,' Gwen replied with a smile. 'We need to go in a few minutes.

Dad, I'm sorry, but us coming to living here when we're married . . . it's not going to happen that way. Thank you for the offer but we have other plans.'

'I see.' He looked crestfallen.

'We'll still come round a lot of the time,' Gwen assured him quickly. 'I can come and cook for you sometimes, and you can come to the flat to eat and spend time with us.'

'Fine,' he replied.

'We'd better be off or we'll be late for the rehearsal.' Adam felt awful that they had to leave.

They set out in the hire car and were the first to arrive at the hall.

'Sorry about that,' Adam muttered. 'I wanted to avoid conflict. I do like your dad, but I'd never thought of us actually living with him. Perhaps it wasn't such a good idea of mine to rush this wedding date.'

Gwen shook her head.

'Don't worry about it. I'd much rather live in your flat. He'll come round.'

The rehearsal was soon underway. They got through the first act without any problems, but the second act was interrupted by Geoffrey's late arrival.

'I've got a surprise for all of you,' he announced from the doorway. 'Ta-da! Here she is. Our little Cindy. She has agreed to come back to us and has even agreed to be our prompt. How about that for a generous offer?'

'Hello, everyone,' Crystal said in her quiet voice.

'Welcome back. We all hope you're feeling much better now.' Paul spoke in his usual actor's voice, sounding most professional. 'And thank you for offering to act as prompt. I'm sure those who've been standing in will be delighted.'

'That's all right. I'll at least be part of it all,' Crystal replied. 'It's not quite the same, but it is better than nothing.'

'Right, let's get on, then, shall we? Act two, please, everyone.'

Things started to go badly after Crystal took over as prompt. She stopped people every time they missed even one word and corrected them. Then she lost her place in the script and asked if they could repeat the previous sentences.

She kept finding fault with Gwen until Gwen couldn't really remember any of her lines. She felt ready to slap the girl for constantly interrupting their progress.

She felt hot and sweaty and wondered how on earth she was going to manage another act. It was all made worse by the insufferable Geoffrey telling Crystal what a wonderful job she was doing.

Adam sat close to Gwen and tried to comfort her.

'I hope Paul will have a word with her.'

'Me, too,' Gwen agreed. 'Geoffrey makes up half his lines and she never says a word about him going wrong.'

'Of course she's going to correct you.

She resents you taking over what she saw as her part. Don't worry about it. If you get stopped too often, Paul is bound to speak to her about it, otherwise it will slow us all down.'

'I know you're right. It's just so difficult when you're the one being targeted.' Gwen sighed.

The next act went considerably better without too many stoppages, largely due to Crystal being bored by this time. They even reached the wedding scene without a massive pause and the couple smiled at each other, thinking of the final performance when they planned to make their own announcement.

'Thank you all very much,' Paul announced. 'I have just a few notes. Sally and Marie, I'd like you to look a bit more horrified when Gwen announces they are to be married. You have some good lines around that point and need to make a bit more of them.'

'We'd love to, but we were told we must check every single word.' Marie glared at Crystal as she spoke.

'Yes, perhaps Crystal was a little over zealous with some of you. It was her first go at doing the prompting. She'll soon get the hang of it and I'm sure we'll be very grateful to her.'

Crystal stood up huffily.

'If you don't like what I'm doing, I can easily manage without it. I'm only doing it to please my dad. He wanted me to take part and this is what I was trying to do.' The girl then burst into tears and everyone sat uncomfortably looking around the room.

'I'm sure you'll get better at the job in a few days,' Paul reassured Crystal. 'I can understand it was difficult the first time. Stay behind and I'll talk to you about what we need from you.'

Paul was trying to be diplomatic and wanted to move on.

'If you don't like me doing this stupid job, I'm going. I can't take all the criticism — especially from some people.' Crystal glared at Gwen and Adam. 'Pity they can't learn their lines properly and save someone from having to correct them all the time. You can keep your wretched drama group. I don't want anything more to do with you lot. Sorry, Dad, I've had enough.' She limped out, making a great show of using her crutches.

Geoffrey ran after her.

'Crystal, darling, please wait a minute. Crystal!'

Margaret, her mother, gave a loud tut and also collected her things and left the hall.

Everyone was silent for a moment then a buzz of chat broke out. Paul coughed loudly and called for quiet.

'I'm sorry about that. Embarrassing all round. I think I'll be looking for another person to prompt — unless you're all going to be word perfect next time.

'Thank you all for your efforts. We have just over two weeks to go, so not much longer. We'll be making a start on the rest of the set tomorrow, so it will be the day after for the next rehearsal.'

The group broke up, feeling somewhat disgruntled. It hadn't been the best of rehearsals and Crystal's outburst had depressed most of the main characters.

Gwen was especially upset, partly because she was usually complimented on how well she had done to catch up with the rest, and partly because she hated to be resented as much as she was by Crystal.

Gwen said very little to anyone and suggested she and Adam should leave without going through to the bar for a drink. Adam accepted her wishes and they went back to her house.

'I'm too weary to discuss anything else tonight,' she told him. 'The business of where we going to live, let's leave it for now.'

Adam nodded.

'OK, love. But we do need to talk it through very soon. It is only a couple of weeks before it all happens. I hope this is all going to work. The play, I mean. It is pretty amateurish at the moment.

Neither one thing nor the other. Perhaps we could turn it into a more modern day sort of pantomime. A bit more slapstick here and there. What do you think?'

'I suppose so. Actually, it might work out better.' Gwen suddenly woke up at the thought of it and began to get excited at the prospect. 'What would we need to do to the play? Make the father more of a comedy character and perhaps add a couple of bailiffs? Good old Geoffrey could be one of them quite easily.'

'Always assuming Geoffrey comes back again after his daughter's outburst.'

'There's no danger he wouldn't come back, is there?' Gwen asked.

'Who knows?' Adam admitted. 'Perhaps he's really taken the huff this time. I doubt he'd let us all down, though. I'm going home now. Give some thought to our idea and let's meet tomorrow and see if there's anything we can suggest to retrieve the play. Night, love. Sleep well.'

'Not much chance of that with all the stuff we have planned.' Gwen laughed. 'The wedding, I mean, as well as the play.'

'I thought we'd organised most of what was needed for the wedding? It's all pretty minimal, isn't it?'

'Yes, of course it is. We only have the problem of where we're going to live and what I'm going to wear. Plus the reception to organise.'

'Come on, love. For the reception, why don't we just order extra stuff from the bakers' shop in town? I don't want you getting exhausted cooking and so on. They'd deliver it here to your place and we can just pick it up from there.'

Gwen sighed.

'Sorry, I know I'm making a stupid fuss. Anyway, night to you, too.' They kissed each other and smiled happily at the thought of their wedding.

★　★　★

Adam drove back home to his flat and let himself in. He booted up his computer and started to work out some ideas. He would have liked to have had the script on the machine, but he sat with it open beside him.

Was it too late to alter this script? What would others think?

He glanced at his watch. It was half past ten. Was it too late to phone Paul?

Hang it, he thought, and picked up his phone and dialled.

Paul's wife answered.

'Hi, it's Adam. I'm sorry to call so late but I need to speak to Paul. Is he available?'

'Yes, I suppose so.' She didn't sound pleased to hear his voice, Adam thought.

He heard her calling for her husband. A few seconds later Paul spoke.

'Hello?'

'Hi, Paul. It's Adam. I've been thinking quite a bit after tonight's rehearsal and I'm wondering if we should make the whole thing more like a traditional pantomime after all. I've been looking through the script and there are lots of places where it can be changed. I don't think it would make it too difficult to change various lines, and let's face it, not everyone has learned their lines yet.'

'Good heavens! You do realise how close we are to the production?'

'Of course. I'm not suggesting major changes,' Adam explained. 'My lines for instance . . . I could play them much more cynically without changing the words at all. Most of it is with Gwen and she'd certainly cope with my ideas.'

'Let me think about it. It's too late to do anything tonight and we don't have a rehearsal tomorrow anyway. I'll call you in the morning.'

'OK. I'll continue to look through the script so I'll have a better idea of what I'm suggesting. Goodnight, Paul.'

Adam sat by his computer and added a few words here and there. He could see it all as a production, and if they put in a few songs here and there, it would liven it up and make it a bit longer, too.

He thought of a band he'd played with a few years ago and wondered if they'd all be willing to come and play as part of this production. He started to make notes, and finally, at about half past three in the morning, he felt he knew exactly what was needed for the play.

He gave a loud yawn and realised he needed to get some sleep. He laid down on his sofa and was soon asleep.

He woke suddenly, realising it was nine-thirty and he was late for work.

He cursed silently. His alarm had gone off at the usual time but he'd been too far away to hear it.

He'd work from home, he decided, and phoned his office. He realised Paul hadn't called him so he tried his number.

'Hello, it's Adam again,' he said to Paul's wife.

'He's not here, I'm afraid. He's gone to the hall. Something about building the set along with some of the others.'

'Thanks very much. I'm sorry to disturb you.'

Adam stared at his computer again and, with a sigh, started on his daily working tasks.

At one o'clock he stopped for something to eat. He decided to call his friend who was one of the people who played in the band.

'Thomas! How are you?'

'Adam? How are you, my friend?'

'I'm good.'

'Still seeing the lovely Gwen?'

'Oh, yes. Very much so. In fact . . . ' He paused. 'We're in the same play, acting opposite each other.'

Phew, he'd nearly given everything away.

'It's about the play I'm calling,' he continued. 'Are you and the boys still playing together?'

'Well, a bit off and on. We meet quite often and have a bit of a jam. We miss you actually. Any chance of you coming back to play with us?'

'Not really. The thing is, we're doing a pantomime and I've had an idea that could involve you. How would you feel about coming and playing a few numbers for us?'

'I'm sure we'd love to, but we're horribly out of practice,' Thomas confessed.

'You've got two weeks to practise. You know the numbers already, but you might need to have one or two of the cast to sing with you. This is all just an idea. I've still to sell it to the rest of the cast. I don't see there being a problem, though.'

'Leave it with me. I'll talk to Dave and James. I'll get back to you later today.'

'Thanks. That's great. Bye now.' Adam switched his phone off and punched the air.

★   ★   ★

During the afternoon, Paul phoned.

'So, tell me about your idea,' he said.

'OK. I was thinking we could still follow the same plan and put in one or two extra bits here and there and make it more like a modern day pantomime,' Adam explained. 'Some music here and there would bring it all to life — and I know just the group who could do this.'

'Sounds as though you're well ahead of me. If you think you can get everyone's agreement, go ahead,' Paul replied. 'I want it all to be a success and at the moment I do have my doubts — and not just Crystal's dreadful outburst last night. That was almost the final straw for me. I still have to talk to Geoffrey and get him back on side. Anyway, the set is progressing so that's something. Where would you be putting this group of yours?'

'Down at the front of the stage. A sort of orchestra pit.' Adam laughed.

'That won't please Mrs Probert. She likes to sit on the front row,' Paul pointed out.

'Then perhaps she'll have to move on this occasion. What shall I do now?'

'Perhaps you could talk to those who are most concerned.'

'OK. I will. Actually, Geoffrey is one of the main people. But as he doesn't remotely know his lines, he'll probably just ad-lib as usual. Marie and Sally and Gwen, of course.' Adam stopped for a moment to think. 'And Jack. If I ask them all to a meeting, do you want to come as well?'

'I'm not sure when I could come. I'll be back at the hall this evening and we'll be making a noise, so it wouldn't be a good place to meet.'

'I'll suggest my place,' Adam said. 'Leave it with me.'

Adam gave up working for the rest of the day and made a series of phone calls. He asked everyone to come to his flat at seven o'clock that evening. They all agreed, despite missing out on an evening off.

He looked in the fridge and decided he needed a few things from the shop. He rushed out and bought some wine and a few packs of nibbles.

By seven-fifteen, the group were all there and wondering why. Adam poured wine for everyone and had put out some crisps and nuts.

'OK, Adam.' Jack was the first to speak. 'What's this all about?'

'Seeing how the rehearsal went last night set me thinking,' Adam began. 'I've discussed it with Paul and he's left it to me to present my ideas. I've called you here as the main people involved. Geoffrey, too, but I was leaving it to Paul to see how the land lies there.

'I thought that this is a more modern pantomime, but that it wouldn't take a lot to turn it into a proper panto. I've worked through the script and added some stuff here and there and I think it could really work.

'It means some of you changing your roles slightly; Sally and Marie particularly. There would be more jokes added. And Jack, you'd play the father with a degree of hopelessness. You know, wringing your hands together because you can't control your daughters' spending habits.'

'I like the sound of it,' Sally told the group.

'Me, too,' Marie added. 'I can really see it all working well. The only thing is, don't we need some music?'

'Remember our local group, the Last Word? Well, I used to be a member. I've approached them and they're willing to be involved. They can sing most of the sort of stuff we'd need. What do you think?'

'I love the idea,' Marie agreed. 'We know most of the play and can always ad-lib if necessary. Unless we get someone who's a stickler for correctness as prompter.'

'Crystal will not be involved any more,' Adam announced firmly. 'Now, if you've got your scripts handy, let's look at adding some bits here and there.'

'How exciting!' Gwen exclaimed. 'I'm looking forward to all of this. It's really going to be much better as a real pantomime.'

'I was thinking we could have a fashion advisor coming in to dress Gwen for the ball, instead of a fairy godmother.' The females all giggled at this suggestion.

'Oh, yes, I love it. Who could play that part?' Gwen asked.

'I wondered about Paul doing it himself,' Adam replied. 'He's certainly got plenty of experience at acting. I haven't asked him yet so don't say anything. I can see him as Gok Wan, can't you?'

'Oh, yes, definitely.'

'Gok what?' Jack asked.

'No, Wan. Gok Wan.'

'What on earth is that?'

The group laughed.

'He's a fashion guru on television. Very outside the box. For goodness' sake, Jack, everybody knows Gok Wan.' Sally laughed.

'Right, shall we get to work?' Adam said.

7

Music to Their Ears

Soon they were all scribbling extra words on to their scripts and several of them were laughing helplessly.

'That's a good sign,' Gwen whispered to Adam, who nodded his agreement.

At last they reached the final act. This was the finale — the wedding scene.

'I suppose we need more costumes instead of the simple idea of a registry office wedding,' Adam told them.

'How about the guests turn up for the ceremony dressed in all sorts of clothes?' Gwen suggested. 'Someone could come in gardening clothes; someone in a cook's outfit. You know the sort of thing. We could add some lines for each of them, interrupting the person doing the wedding. It could be quite amusing, don't you think?' Gwen was getting carried away by her idea.

'Lines like 'We'd heard there was something going on so came to see what it was'?' Adam added his piece.

'OK, let's go with that.'

Lots more scribbling went on until everyone was present at the wedding and they all laughed at their final effort. They talked about music and decided they'd all sing together as a final song. They couldn't decide what it might be at this stage, but decided Adam should discuss it with the band.

'Wow, that was such a good night's work,' Adam said to the group. 'Thank you, everyone. Now go and learn your new lines. I'll talk to Paul tomorrow and persuade him to play Gok.'

* * *

Adam slept like a log. He was exhausted by his efforts of the previous evening as well as his working day, though he did feel guilty that he hadn't worked a full day. Thank goodness it was Friday the next day.

He called Paul in the morning before he went to work.

'I've got a favour to ask of you, Paul,' he began. 'Would you be willing to play a role? Only a small one. Not a huge amount to learn or anything.'

Paul hesitated.

'Well, I'm not sure it's a good idea, what with me directing and all that.'

'I'm sure you could fit it in. We'd like you to play Gok Wan, the fashion guru. We can come up with a different name, of course, but it's based on him. A very over the top sort of character. What do you say?'

'I suppose so. I gather your ideas went down well last night? I was planning to come round but it got rather late before we finished.'

'All went very well,' Adam assured him. 'How did you get on with Geoffrey?'

'Difficult. He was very upset about our treatment of his daughter. He thought we were being unfair to her.'

'She was pretty unfair to most of us. Anyway, is he still going to be in the play?'

'I think so. He won't like it if you give him too many changes in the script, though.'

'It will be no more than he'll cause himself by forgetting his own lines. No, there will be no real changes for him. I'd better get off to work now. See you this evening, Gok.'

'I'll think about it,' Paul replied with a laugh. He actually sounded quite pleased with the outcome.

⋆　⋆　⋆

There was a definite air of anticipation at the rehearsal that evening. It seemed the entire cast had heard of the changes that were being proposed.

'What a ridiculous idea. Why on earth are we changing everything at this stage?' This was Mrs Probert's contribution.

Paul stood up and asked for silence.

'As you all seem to have heard, we are proposing to add more humour to our performance and make it into more of a proper pantomime. It will attract more younger people and make it much more of a traditional Christmas production.

'The main changes have been explained to those involved, and the rest of you will find your lines remain pretty much as they were. We're also going to include a band, who will be with us next week.'

Paul took a breath before continuing.

'Now, as you all realise, time is of the essence. We have two weeks till the dress rehearsal. I'm sure we can all manage to adapt. Let's begin tonight's proceedings with Act One, Scene One. Thank you all for listening.'

There was a buzz of excited anticipation and the rehearsal got underway. Soon everyone was laughing. Everyone agreed the whole play had been lifted to a different place.

Halfway through the rehearsal, Geoffrey turned up.

'Sorry to be late, everyone. Poor Crystal's had another accident and we were stuck at Casualty. I tell you, Casualty here is nothing like the television series.

'Sorry, were you in the middle of something?' He was responding to the sight of everyone standing looking at him.

'We're in the middle of the rehearsal, Geoffrey,' Paul told him curtly. 'You'll be on in a few minutes. Right, everyone. Go from the top of the page.'

Geoffrey spoke again.

'Sorry and all that. Forget I'm here. Crystal's going to be all right, by the way. She had to have a new plaster put on, poor kid. She had a serious fall. We haven't yet found out all the details. Something to do with that wretched boyfriend of hers. What's his name? Rocky something or other. Apparently he . . . '

'Can we hear about it later, please, Geoffrey? We do need to press on with this rehearsal.' Paul was beginning to get angry.

'Sorry,' he said, raising his hand. 'Ignore me.'

'OK, back to the top of the page.'

They jolted along. The flow was disturbed and several of the cast members forgot their lines.

'Come on now, people. Get it together, please,' Paul urged.' Let's take a short break and then get back to a proper rehearsal. Just over two weeks is all we've got.'

They broke up for a while and chatted amongst themselves. They were taking it in turns to prompt. Anyone who wasn't in a scene would do the job and then someone else would take over. It was far from satisfactory.

'I wonder if my dad would do it?' Gwen said suddenly to Adam. 'He's sitting at home on his own anyway. It might do him some good to get out. What do you think?'

'It might work.' Adam nodded. 'You could always ask him. We certainly need someone. Otherwise it's Mrs Parkinson or Mrs Probert. Can you just imagine either of them doing it?'

Gwen laughed.

'Er, no. That would be even worse than Crystal. Poor girl.'

'I wonder what she was doing to crack her plaster.'

'Goodness knows,' Gwen replied thoughtfully. 'I still wonder about that Rocky. I think he may have been involved in your car theft. Has anything happened about that yet?'

'I haven't attempted to ask as yet. Let's face it, I've been a bit busy with this play, not to mention working.'

'Perhaps you should call the police tomorrow?' Gwen suggested.

Before Adam had a chance to reply, Paul had interrupted.

'Right, everyone. Let's get going again. The three girls on stage, please. The rest of you, try to be silent as you watch. It is very disconcerting to have lots of chatter going on in the background.' Paul was getting back into his director's role.

By the time they reached the end of

the play, they all felt exhausted.

'We'll have the band here next week,' Paul promised them. 'I gather they're planning exactly what we need over the weekend. Is that right, Adam?'

Adam nodded.

'Yes. We've set tomorrow aside for rehearsals and anyone involved in a singing role, I'll contact on Sunday. Maybe you can come round for a practice then, too. I'll let you know anyway.'

'Excellent.'

'I'm not sure I've heard about any band,' Geoffrey put in, frowning. 'Is this a new idea?'

'Oh, catch up, Geoffrey,' one of the others said. 'We're doing a proper panto now. You have to have music in a panto.'

'Oh, are we? I didn't realise. What will be different?'

'Your part stays much the same as it's always been,' Paul told him. 'Different costume and title. Didn't you realise things have changed since the last rehearsal?'

'I just thought people were improvising a bit more.' He smiled benignly as everyone sighed in exasperation. 'I'm about ready for a drink. Anyone else?'

'I'd like to spend some time with you Gwen, working on the . . . Well, I'll call it the transformation scene,' Paul replied. 'Have you got some time over the weekend?'

Gwen nodded.

'Sure. I won't be involved in the band rehearsal, so whenever you like.'

'Excellent. Tomorrow afternoon, shall we say?'

'Fine.'

'Come round to our place. We should be able to get it all sorted then.'

'No problem. Around two-thirty?' Gwen suggested.

'Excellent.'

'By the way, I wondered if I should ask my dad to come and prompt. What do you think?' she asked as an afterthought.

'That would be marvellous,' Paul

agreed enthusiastically. 'Do you think he would?'

'I can probably persuade him. It would do him good to get out occasionally and meet people. I know he's not actually a member, but I guess that wouldn't really matter.'

'Not at all. Anyone willing to prompt would be welcome. We can't go on like we did tonight,' Paul admitted.

'Leave it with me,' Gwen replied. 'I'll tell him how urgent it is and he won't be able to say no. I'll see you tomorrow, hopefully with some good news.'

★   ★   ★

At last Gwen found Adam again and they drove back to his flat.

'I need to go home and talk to Dad. I'm going to ask him to prompt. Fingers crossed for me.'

'He'll say yes, I'm sure, once you've explained to him what it entails,' Adam replied. 'Don't tell him what an awful task it is or he'll definitely say no. Tell

100

him how much we all look forward to having him with us.'

'Oh, I will, don't worry. I'd better get going now or he'll be in bed. Good luck with your band tomorrow.'

'Good luck to you with Paul, too. I just hope it all works out.'

★ ★ ★

Adam sat at his computer for another couple of hours, looking at various pieces of music he knew the band had played before. Hopefully they would be able to find some songs from the past without having to learn much that was new to them.

He had played bass guitar with the group and still remembered a lot of their music. He felt certain it was all going to work out well. He might even dig out his own guitar and play along with the band.

He went to bed with his mind racing with ideas, most of which kept him awake for much of the night.

* * *

At ten o'clock the next morning, Adam went to the hall where the band had planned to meet him. They arrived around half past ten, looking somewhat the worse for wear.

'Sorry, mate,' Thomas apologised. 'We had an unexpected gig last night and didn't get to bed till rather late. So, what are you thinking of?'

'We thought you could set up down here,' Adam replied, indicating the area. 'Then you would have a good view of the stage and see who is about to sing. There's only a couple of numbers for soloists. The rest will be you singing and playing. How does that sound?'

'Fine. As long as you're happy with older stuff. We don't really have much time to come up with anything new.'

'Absolutely.' Adam then went on to list some of the numbers he thought would fit into the theme of the play, and mentioned the song he would sing with Gwen.

'That sounds fine.' Thomas nodded. 'Shall we run through them now?'

'Why not? Let's start with 'Fed Up And Lonely'. This could be sung as the background to Cindy feeling low about all the things her sisters are doing and saying to her.'

Adam had already explained the plot to the boys so they knew exactly what he was talking about.

They began to play, with Dave doing the vocals.

'Do you want us to use our own mikes and stuff?' Dave asked once the number was over.

Adam frowned.

'I hadn't really thought about it. I suppose so, though we don't want it too loud as you're pretty close to the audience. That was good. It makes me somewhat nostalgic for my days with the band.'

'Nothing to stop you coming back,' Thomas teased. 'You've still got your bass, haven't you?'

'Yes, but I don't have enough time

103

these days. I don't think Gwen would go with it, either,' Adam admitted.

'Are you two engaged yet?' Thomas asked.

'Nothing formal yet.'

'Don't wait too long or I might make a pitch for her myself.'

Adam laughed.

'Don't even think of it. She's mine and don't you forget it,' he warned good-naturedly. 'Anyway, I do plan to sing with you if not actually play.'

'That's great. Let us know which song and we can accompany you in fine style.'

'I thought I'd do one of our oldies. 'Lovin' You is Easy', for example.'

'Good choice. Come on, lads.' James started with a few chords and soon they were all singing along.

'Definitely that one,' James said cheerfully. 'What else? 'Feelin' Lonely'? That should fit in somewhere, I'm sure.'

They started playing that one and soon they all joined in again.

'OK, you've made your point.' Adam laughed. 'I'm not saying I'll come back, but an occasional performance as a guest may well be possible.'

He went on through his list and used his script to illustrate points when they could do some sound effects: mostly drum beats and symbol crashes.

By lunchtime, they'd covered the entire list.

'The next rehearsal is on Monday,' Adam told them. 'Can you all be here for that? We can then set it to work properly, in the right order.'

They all agreed.

'I'll see if we can get some payment to cover expenses, but it won't be much, I'm afraid,' Adam told them.

'No worries,' Thomas assured him. 'It's all good experience. Not everyone plays for the most prestigious pantomime in Cornwall.'

'We're not quite that, but thanks anyway.' Adam laughed. 'I think we've covered most things. Any questions?'

'I think we're all set, aren't we?' The

band murmured their agreement and, with a shake of hands, they cleared their stuff and disappeared.

★ ★ ★

Adam wondered whether to go to Paul's house to see how they were getting on, but decided to leave them to it. Instead, he called at the supermarket and bought some supplies, including a pasty.

He munched it while sitting in his hire car, then realised he'd done nothing about getting a new car. He would phone his insurance company and maybe the police, too, when he got home.

He dialled the police first of all to enquire about progress. There was none. He then dialled his insurance company to ask about what he needed to do. Again, it seemed there was nothing.

'You can keep using your hire car until we get a report from the police. After that, we'll see what we can do.'

Adam felt somewhat disconcerted but tried to relax, knowing there was nothing more he could do about it.

He wanted to see Gwen. He missed her. In just over two weeks, they would be married. They'd been together for three years now so it was high time they made it official.

He really hoped she was happy about the situation and began to feel guilty that he might have rushed her into his crazy idea. He knew that every girl dreamed of a lovely wedding with a long dress and her favourite people there at the ceremony. What had he done?

He needed to talk it through with her. He called her mobile but got no answer. She had obviously turned it off while they were working.

★　★　★

At Paul's house, Gwen was shyly talking about the traditional transformation scene.

'It's usual for a fairy godmother to arrive, wave her wand a few times and then Cindy's ready for the ball. As we're not having a ball as such, what do you think?' she asked. 'There will be a disco sort of dance. I'm not even sure what she would want to wear for that. What do you think?'

'I could be your Fairy Gok Mother,' Paul suggested and Gwen laughed.

'Oh, I like that!' she said.

'I've been looking him up on the website. He does lots more than fashion. He does cooking and home makeovers, too. All sorts.'

Gwen nodded.

'OK. Let's pretend Cindy has written to him and has been picked out for a home visit. He could come in with various pots and pans and start trying to cook. Then he could look at the state of the home and decide to do a home makeover. What do you think?'

'Sounds good,' Gwen agreed. 'You could then say you want to go to the disco and he changes his plans to find a suitable outfit for you. I think this definitely has promise. Let's give it a bit of a run through.'

'How on earth shall we start?'

'You're feeling sad to be left behind after everyone else has left. You're sitting by the fire staring into it.'

'OK.' Gwen nodded. 'You then knock at the door and bounce in.'

'Hi, there,' Paul replied as Gok Wan. 'Are you the owner of the house? I'm here to show you how to cook the most amazing meal using Gok's wok.'

'You're Gok Wan!'

'Yes, indeed. You've recognised me. Wonderful.'

'But what are you doing here?' Cindy replied.

'Didn't you write to me?' Gok returned. 'Inviting me to call in?'

'Me? I'm sorry, no.' Cindy was confused. 'It must have been one of my stepsisters. They're always writing to someone or other.'

Gok looked around, shaking his head.

'It looks to me as if you need more than someone to cook for you. This place needs a total makeover. Maybe we could do that for you, too.'

'I'd really like a makeover for me, please!' Cindy told him, sounding excited. 'I want to go the most exclusive disco there's ever been in the area. My stepsisters are there and a band called the Last Word are also playing. It'll be wonderful. But I'm stuck at home. Anyway, I've nothing to wear . . . '

At this point Cindy burst into tears.

Gwen began to giggle as Paul did a performance of moving round her, using his hands to make frames and holding them up in front of her. He had even produced some large spectacles to complete his character and he kept peering through them as if she were some strange specimen.

They worked on for another hour until they felt it would work the way they wanted it to.

'I think that should about do it, don't you?' Paul asked.

'I think it will be great!' Gwen gushed. 'You're very good.'

'Well, thanks. I have been acting, albeit as an amateur, for rather a long time,' Paul said modestly. 'I do think this will be one of my favourite roles, however. Besides, I don't have to learn too much. With just the two of us, we can ad-lib as much as we like.'

'I'll take your word for it, Mr Director,' Gwen said with a laugh. 'I must go now. Adam will think I've got lost.'

'Thanks for your input,' Paul said. 'Have a nice evening.'

'Bye, then. See you on Monday.'

★ ★ ★

Gwen drove home and then called Adam.

'How did it go?' he asked.

'Really well. Paul's very good. What are you doing?'

'Nothing. I need to see you to talk. Will you come over?' Adam asked. 'We can do something this evening. I'm not sure what but at least we can be together.'

'I'll come in a little while. I've got a few things to do here and I need to talk to Dad about doing the prompting. I didn't see him last night and he was out fishing this morning. I'll be over about six, is that OK?'

'OK. Shall we go out to eat or shall I cook something here?' Adam asked.

'Let's go out. I feel like doing something. Cinema?'

'OK, I'll see what's on. See you about six.'

It was only just over an hour to wait. He could find something to do till then.

Adam slumped down on his sofa and promptly fell asleep. He was woken when Gwen came into the room and spoke to him.

'Hello, sleepyhead.' She kissed him and sat down beside him. 'So, what have you found for us to do?'

'Sorry I fell asleep. The band were great. I really think it will all work out perfectly. I'm going to do a couple of numbers with them. Old ones, of course. We have no time to put in anything new. They're coming to Monday's rehearsal,' he informed her.

'You'll be able to see me and my Fairy Gok Mother.'

Adam laughed.

'Who came up with that one?'

'Paul, of course.' Gwen smiled. 'Anyway, you wanted to talk to me?'

'Yes. It's about the wedding . . . '

8

The Search is On

Gwen stared at Adam. She gave a shiver. He looked so serious and a bit upset. Surely he hadn't changed his mind?

'I see. What do you want to say?'

'I've been thinking. Most girls look forward to their wedding day and spend months planning it all down to the smallest detail. The dress, who they'll invite, flowers and a million other little things. I've talked you into a minimal ceremony with no-one else coming to wish us well, and you don't even know what you're going to wear. I feel desperately guilty.'

Gwen frowned.

'And you don't want to go ahead with it? Is that it?'

Adam shook his head.

'Of course not. I want to be married to you more than anything. But I'm not sure it's what you want,' he said softly.

'You are an idiot. I'd never have said yes if it wasn't what suits me. Since Mum died I've always dreaded my wedding day. Without her to get excited beside me, it's hung over me.

'Your idea has given me exactly what I wanted,' Gwen went on. 'I didn't know it at the time, but once you suggested it, I knew it was right.'

Adam felt a load lifted from his shoulders and gave her a big grin.

'My darling Gwen, thank you so much. I promise we'll have a really good reception with the gang. Any relations you need to ask — we can see them later and have another party. I might even dig up the odd ancient aunt or two to join in.'

'Oh, poor Adam. I never thought about you being on your own. You've always had so many friends that I forgot about your lack of relatives.'

'I do actually have a brother,' Adam

said quietly. 'I haven't seen him for yonks, though.'

'You've got an actual brother?' She was amazed. 'I can't believe you've never told me that before!'

'We lost touch before I went to university. I don't really talk about him to anyone.'

'What does he do?'

'I don't know. He was in the Army. He left home long before our parents died. He came back for their funerals but then he disappeared again.'

'And you've never bothered to find him again?'

Adam shrugged.

'What's the point? He has his own life and left me behind with my parents. Then they were both killed in the crash and everything was eventually sold and the proceeds divided. At least I bought my flat and kept a bit of cash back for emergencies.'

Gwen was sitting quietly, with tears in her eyes.

'Hey, no crying allowed!' Adam said

brightly. 'I'm not bothered. Really I'm not.'

'But there's so much I don't know about you.' Gwen sobbed. 'I really can't believe you've never told me about this brother of yours. What's his name?'

'Rory.'

'Rory Jerrold. Wouldn't you like to find him and invite him to our wedding?'

'Heavens, no! I have no idea where he is. I have no idea what he's done with his life, whether he's married or not, got a family — nothing. He's never bothered about me so why should I bother about him? Now, do you want to go out to eat?'

Gwen was quiet for a moment, digesting what she'd just been told. How could he bear to know he had a brother whom he never saw or heard about? If it had been her, she could never have ignored the idea at all.

'Gwen?'

'Sorry, what did you say?'

'I asked if you wanted to go out to eat.'

'I don't mind. Have you looked him up on the web?'

'Who? Oh, Rory, you mean. I did once but no joy. So, eat out or stay in?'

Gwen considered.

'Oh, let's go out. We can chat over a meal just as easily as if we stay in.'

'Where shall we go?' Adam asked. 'I could treat us to something posh or we could go to a pub. What do you fancy?'

'Pub, I think. I'm not exactly dressed for anywhere posh.' Gwen smiled.

'OK, pub it is. Let's go to the seaside somewhere. It seems silly living by the sea and never looking at it.'

They drove to a village a couple of miles away and settled down in the pub.

A band were playing so the plan to talk was somewhat lost. They ate their food, their feet tapping away, and enjoyed themselves.

Gwen noticed a couple of blokes staring at them from one corner of the bar.

'Do you know who they are?' she asked Adam. 'The couple of chaps standing near the bar.'

Adam turned to look.

'Not really. They look like some of the local lads who hang around the market place at home, but I'm not sure.'

The pair nudged each other and were smiling in a rather sinister way.

'I don't like it,' Gwen told him. 'They scare me a bit.'

'Don't let them. It wouldn't surprise me if it was them or some of their mates who burned my car.'

'Heavens!' Gwen exclaimed. 'They really do look sort of seedy. Let's finish our drinks and go home.'

'OK. I wonder if they are from our village. They do look familiar, but then, they are of a type. I'll go and pay anyway and we'll go.'

He went to the bar and asked for their bill.

While he was there, one of the two men went over to Gwen.

'Hello, darlin',' he said.

'What do you want?' she asked, slightly nervous.

'You're in that drama group, back in town, aren't you?'

'So?'

'You know Crystal?'

'Well, yes. Slightly.'

'She's well hacked off with someone who took over her part in the play. I'd watch out if I were you.'

Gwen was shocked and looked desperately around to see if Adam was coming back to the table.

'Go away, please,' she begged. 'Leave me alone. My fiancé will be back in a minute and he won't be too pleased to hear you threatening me.'

'Threatening you, darlin'?' The man sneered. 'Nothing could be further from the truth. Unless it's you who took over our friend Crystal's part. Could it be you?'

'It's nothing to do with you. Now go away, please.'

'Go away, please,' he mocked. 'Always

nice and polite to say please.'

He noticed Adam coming back and smiled sweetly at Gwen before going back to his corner. He and his mate giggled together as they watched the pair.

'Nighty-night, darlin',' he called out as they were leaving.

'What was all that about?' Adam asked. He hadn't noticed the previous conversation while he had been paying.

Gwen started to cry.

'He was definitely threatening me, Adam.' She sniffed. 'He asked me if I knew Crystal and if I'd taken over her part in the play. He said she was very upset about losing the part. Oh, Adam, he really scared me.'

'Should I go back and challenge him? I really don't like you being upset.'

'No, please don't. He's likely to attack you,' Gwen pleaded.

'I can defend myself.'

'But there are two of them. It makes even the drama group seem an unpleasant place to go to, doesn't it?'

'Don't let them worry you,' Adam reassured her. 'They are so bored they don't know what to do with themselves and take up this aggression. Do you want me to call the police? Maybe I should if you think they might have been involved with my car theft.'

Gwen shook her head.

'I don't have any proof. It wouldn't work. Poor Crystal — fancy knowing these types. I can't imagine Geoffrey being that pleased at her association.'

★ ★ ★

They stopped outside his flat and Adam suggested now was perhaps the time to talk.

They went inside and he put the kettle on for coffee. He felt slightly disturbed at the memory of the two yobs they'd seen in the pub. He was particularly disturbed at the thought that one of them had talked to Gwen the way he had.

'I'm still not happy about those two

we saw in the pub,' he told her. 'I'm wondering if I should tell the police after all.'

'I'd just leave it for now,' Gwen replied. 'They aren't very nice people, but there's nothing to say they'd actually do any damage. They might be full of threats, but that's about all they'll do.'

'I hope you're right. My car, for instance?'

'We don't know it was them.'

'I suppose not. Seems likely, though, doesn't it? I mean the connection with Crystal and various other things they said.'

Gwen stared into space. She didn't want to think about them doing anything awful and instead changed the subject.

'So, where are we going to live once we're married?' she asked suddenly.

'Oh, I don't know. I know what your dad means about him having the room, but I've got used to this place and I want you to myself, not sharing someone else's home.' Adam hesitated. 'Will he be very upset if we stay here? I don't want to upset him.'

'I really don't know,' Gwen admitted. 'He was talking about redecorating the spare bedroom and making it into a sort of sitting-room for us. I really don't know how it would work out.'

Adam sat thinking about the idea. He knew it went against everything he was thinking about. He saw them starting married life in his flat, then moving to a larger place, perhaps, when — if — they were lucky enough to have a baby.

He gave a shiver. It was something he had never really thought about, but the idea was lurking there. They were both nearing thirty so it must be on the cards at some point before too long.

'I'm really not sure, either,' Adam replied. 'Can we start out living here and see how it goes? This place is paid for so living expenses won't cost all that much. We're very lucky to have this sort of choice.'

'I know that. The thing is, Dad's not

all that old. He might find another partner anyway and then we'd be in the way.'

'I hadn't thought of that. Is it likely?' Gwen shook her head thoughtfully.

'Not unless he starts to go out a bit more. Perhaps if we don't move in with him he'll get a bit more lonely then see about finding himself someone to share his life. He's been on his own for such a long time, relying on me to look after him.'

'It sounds like we'd be doing him a favour if we didn't move in. I really want to stay here, but if you do want to move there, I won't complain too much.'

'Thank you, love.' Gwen smiled.

'Of course, we do need to think about having a family,' he began, staring at her to see her reaction. 'We're both getting on a bit now.'

'I suppose we are.' Gwen considered. 'Not for a while yet, though. What do you think?'

'Probably. We don't want to wait too

long, though. We need to be young enough to enjoy them.'

'Them? You want more than one?' Gwen teased.

'Well, yes. I'd certainly like more than one.'

'There's only one bedroom in this place,' Gwen pointed out.

'We can look at buying somewhere larger in time,' Adam countered. 'I bought what suited me after my parents died. I could afford something larger, but at the time this was all I needed. My brother had a similar amount of money and I've no idea what he did with his money.'

Gwen nodded.

'Fascinating. I find it hard to believe you've got a brother. Where's he based?'

'I don't know.'

'Don't you care about him?'

Adam looked thoughtful.

'Well, yes, I suppose so,' he admitted. 'We were never all that close. He did take me to my first pop concert before he was posted to wherever it was.

Eventually I went off to university and then my parents were killed. Rory disappeared soon after the funeral and that was it.

'Like I said, I don't think he wants to be in touch with me, and I don't particularly need him in my life,' he continued. 'Anyway, what do you think about us buying a house? We could look for something after the play.'

'Your flat will do for a start anyway,' Gwen decided. 'I can't believe it. Me, a married woman in just a couple of weeks! I must go shopping for a dress soon. And we really need to decide what to order in the way of food for the reception. I think I should go home and start making some lists.'

Adam smiled fondly at his fiancée. She loved her lists and always seemed to work better when she had a few on the go.

Gwen left him and went home to her dad. Adam switched on the television and sank down to surf the channels.

He found an old movie he'd seen

before, many years ago. He'd seen it with the rest of his family before Rory left home and he smiled.

He pushed his fingers through his hair and thought how his mother would say it was time he got it cut. That wouldn't do at all for his current role in the play. He needed to look the part of someone in the music trade.

⋆　⋆　⋆

It was Sunday morning and Adam stretched when he awoke.

He really needed to put some washing on and possibly to clean up the flat a bit, but he rolled over and settled back to sleep some more.

The phone rang and he reached for it.

'Hello.'

'Mr Jerrold? This is Sergeant Chadwick. We're no nearer finding the culprits for the damage done to your car unfortunately, but we're putting it on the back burner for the moment, and we think you should be looking at replacing it.

'If you speak to your insurance company and refer them to us for confirmation, it should all go through quite easily,' Sergeant Chadwick finished.

'I see,' Adam replied unhappily. 'Thank you. I'll call them tomorrow and get something set up.'

'All right then, sir. Have a good day.'

'Thanks.'

Adam put the phone down and sighed. Now that he was thoroughly awake, it really was time to get up and do some of his tasks.

★   ★   ★

Meanwhile Gwen was already up and about and she sat down with a coffee and a pad of paper. She began to work on her lists.

At the top of one, she had written: 'Find out about Rory'.

She had her laptop out and typed his

name into a search engine. Five results came up.

Having looked through them carefully, it seemed that only two could possibly be the Rory she was looking for. One of them was living in Northern England and the other one living abroad somewhere. She wondered what to do and decided to talk to her father about it.

'Dad, what do you think?'

'About what?'

'Well, Adam's just told me he's got a brother and I've looked up his name and found two possible people who could be the one. Should I tell Adam? Or should I contact them?'

'I don't know, love. Maybe send them an e-mail? Then at least you'd know if it was the right person.'

'I thought of that, but felt a bit worried about giving my e-mail address out,' Gwen admitted. 'I could always change my name if necessary. You know, get a different e-mail address. I'll need to anyway once we're married. I can hardly stay as Gwen Harper, can I?'

'Whatever you like, love. Think I might turn in now. Nothing on telly I want to see.'

'Have you thought any more about prompting for the play?' she asked. 'We'd be ever so grateful.'

Her dad frowned.

'I don't know. I'd probably be awful and make a right mess of it.'

'Rubbish. You can read perfectly well.'

'I'll think about it and let you know in the morning.' He stopped at the door and smiled at his daughter. 'How are you doing with your wedding lists? If you need any help, you've only to ask, you know.'

'Thanks, Dad. I'm getting there. It's going to be a very quiet affair as I said. I'm going to look for a dress tomorrow and see a florist about my bouquet.'

'I'm sorry you don't have your mother to help you. She would have loved to be part of all the plans for your big day.'

'Oh, Dad,' Gwen said, getting up from her chair. She flung her arms round her dad and together they both shed a few tears.

'Doing it like this makes it so much easier,' she assured him. 'When I see how some of my colleagues sweat buckets over preparations, I'm so glad I don't have to.'

'He's a good lad, your Adam. I know he'll look after you.'

9

The Perfect Outfit

It was a somewhat frustrating morning
for Gwen. She drove to the nearest
town and began her search for a dress.
She began to wish she had someone
with her to help her choose, but that
would mean letting someone else into
the secret.

She tried several outfits on and
decided against them all. She discarded
blues, greens and yellows and she
definitely didn't want white.

It was nearly lunchtime and she went
to a small café and ordered coffee and a
sandwich. She was sitting thinking
about her miserable failure to find
anything when she spotted an old
friend across the room. It was someone
she had worked with on and off, and
she came over to Gwen.

'Fancy seeing you here,' she said. 'I'd have thought this was a bit off the beaten track for you.'

Gwen smiled.

'I'm just doing some shopping, though I'm not having much success so far,' she replied.

'What are you looking for?'

'Oh, just a smart outfit.'

'Are you going somewhere nice?' her friend asked.

Gwen shook her head. She didn't want to give too much away.

'Not really.'

'Have you tried Cardiman? Not many people know about it. It's down by the river. It's only a small shop but she does have some lovely things.'

'No, I haven't even heard of it. I'll give it a try.'

They chatted about general things and at last she said she must go. Gwen was quite pleased. It was tricky to talk about why she needed this outfit without actually saying why. Luckily, she had managed it.

She paid her bill and left the café, turning down a narrow street and looking for the shop. She spotted it just off the main street. It wasn't easy to find and would never make a fortune, she thought.

She opened the door and went inside.

'Wow!' she exclaimed, seeing the rows of beautiful dresses and trouser suits.

'That's a nice response.' The assistant smiled. 'Can I help you?'

'Can I have a little look first? What an amazing collection — so colourful, and what gorgeous fabrics. Wherever do you find them?'

'I have a contact in the Far East and a local lady who makes them up for me. I design them myself and she makes them to my design,' the girl replied.

'What a talented pair you must be. Oh, I do like this one!' Gwen exclaimed, picking out a bright floral dress with a tiny jacket made of contrasting lilac fabric to pick out one of the floral colours. Was it a wedding outfit, though?

'Why not try it?' the girl offered, indicating the small changing room at the back of the little shop. 'It is slightly more expensive than some of our lines but I'm sure it would look good on you. Are you going to Ascot or something? It would be ideal for that.'

Gwen shook her head.

'It would just be a special occasion dress. I'd love to try it.'

She went into the small cubicle and, almost trembling, she slipped her clothes off and put on this lovely creation. It fitted perfectly and looked lovely.

This was the one, she knew. She slipped the jacket on and did a twirl. The fabric stirred and fell back into perfect place.

It must be silk, she realised, but it was a perfect weight for the design. The woman obviously knew what she was doing. She could change into it for the party and knew she'd raise a few eyebrows.

She glanced at the price tag and gave a gulp. She knew her dad had offered to pay for it, but it did seem a little as if she was playing on that. Never mind, she could always pay half of it.

'How is it?' the assistant asked.

'Beautiful. It fits perfectly.'

'Come and show me,' she invited and Gwen pulled the curtain open.

'That is perfect.' The assistant nodded. 'Have you got shoes to go with it? You should have lilac court shoes. I'd like to take a photo of you in that dress. Would you mind?'

'Oh, please don't,' Gwen begged. 'It's a secret, you see. I don't want anyone to see it for a couple of weeks. I will send you a photo of me wearing it later on, I promise.'

'I see.' The girl gave a knowing smile. 'I'll look forward to it. You will look a dream. Don't you want to try anything else? We've got several different outfits you might like.'

Gwen shook her head.

'No. This is the one. It's gorgeous. Is it made of silk?'

'Yes. The jacket is a slub silk and the dress a medium weight so it flows out when you move. It does look lovely on you and I'm not just saying that to make a sale.' The girl laughed modestly.

'It wouldn't matter if you were. I love it anyway and I'm going to have it.' Gwen felt very determined, especially after her frustrating morning. She changed and handed the dress and jacket back to the assistant for her to wrap up.

Clutching a large bag, she started back towards the car. It had been a very successful day. She had decided she wouldn't have a bouquet after all. There was enough floral content in the dress.

Once home, Gwen hung her new purchase carefully in the wardrobe, covering it with a bag she had saved from something else. Her dad was due home soon and would want to see it, but she was determined to keep him in the dark till nearer the time.

'Hello, Gwen, I'm home!' he called out as he came in. 'Where are you?'

'Coming,' she said as she ran down the stairs.

'How did you get on at the shops?'

'Not bad.' She tried to be casual but her grin gave her away.

'I take it you found something to wear for the wedding?' he asked with a knowing smile.

'Yes, I did, Dad. It's fabulous.'

'Where is it, then? Come on. I need to see it. Go and put it on.'

All her thoughts of keeping it to herself flew out of the window and she ran upstairs and quickly changed. It was the sort of dress that made you do that.

As Gwen walked into the room, her father gasped.

'I've never seen you look so gorgeous!' he exclaimed. 'What a perfect choice for you. Well done, darling.'

'The only snag is that it was rather expensive,' she confessed. 'But I'll pay half. I really couldn't leave it in the shop, could I?'

Her dad laughed.

'Don't be silly. This is your wedding dress. Of course I'll pay for it, and I'll also contribute to whatever you're planning for the reception — or should I say the party — afterwards. I'm getting quite excited.'

'So why not come along with me to the rehearsal and get to know people?' Gwen suggested and her dad nodded.

'OK, I'll come with you. I'm not sure what I have to do.'

'It's easy. You just have to follow the script and if someone forgets their lines, you give them a prompt. Sometimes people will start a speech several pages further on, so at this stage you need to stop them and put them right.' She started to head for the stairs. 'Anyway, I'll go and change and then think about supper.'

Just then there was a knock at the door.

'Heavens, who is that? Can you get it,

Dad? I don't want anyone to see me in my wedding outfit.' She ran upstairs again and went into her bedroom.

It was Adam, so she did well not to be seen. She quickly changed back into her ordinary clothes and went down again.

'Hi, darling. How was your shopping day?' Adam asked.

'Excellent. I got everything I needed and feel very pleased with it.'

Adam hugged her.

'Terrific. I wondered if you'd like to grab something to eat before the rehearsal?'

'Dad's coming, too,' she told him. 'He's agreed to prompt, so perhaps he could join us. I haven't even thought what we're going to eat. What do you think, Dad?'

'If I won't be in the way, I'd love to join you,' he replied. 'There's a few things we need to discuss.'

Adam made a face at Gwen behind her dad's back. He had the feeling it was going to be about them living here instead of at his flat. He really didn't want that and was prepared to say so.

They drove to a small restaurant in town and parked easily. It was still early enough to avoid most people who came to eat there.

Once they had ordered, Gwen's father began to speak.

'I know I asked you if you'd like to stay at my house . . . ' he began.

'We really . . . ' Adam began.

'No, listen to what I have to say. I don't think it would be a good idea, after all,' Gwen's dad admitted. 'You need your own space and somewhere you can be yourselves without having to think about anyone else. So, I'm withdrawing that offer. I think you should move into Adam's flat, Gwen. It may be small, but no doubt you'll be looking for somewhere larger in due course. That's what I wanted to say.'

Gwen reached over to hug him.

'Oh, Dad, thank you for being so understanding. You're quite right. It's what we both want to do.'

'Thank you very much,' Adam added. 'Oh, good. Here comes the food.'

The conversation was fairly light during the time they were eating. Gwen seemed to be very excited so Adam asked her why.

She gave a shrug and told him she was simply looking forward to their wedding. He smiled and looked at her slightly oddly.

'I'm not sure what is exciting you, but I'm happy you're happy. We must plan what we're going to offer everyone at the buffet. I haven't a clue about that, but I'm sure you'll know.'

'I'll make a list,' Gwen stated.

'You and your lists!' Adam laughed. 'And what about a honeymoon? Are we going to have one? Where would you like to go?'

'That's too many questions. Let's think about that side of things later,' Gwen replied. 'It'll be Christmas a week after the wedding. I want us to have a Christmas at home. We could go away after that if you like. I really like that idea.'

Adam nodded.

'OK, we'll plan to go away for the New Year. I'd think a weekend in Blackpool would suit, what do you think?'

Gwen's dad frowned.

'I think you should do something more special than that,' he said.

'He's having you on!' Gwen giggled. 'Take no notice of him.'

'What a cheek!' Adam laughed. 'Now, have you both finished? Only we need to make a move. The lads from the band are coming tonight to see how they fit into the show. I need to be there on time to see them in.'

'Yes, of course. I'm looking forward to seeing them again. It's ages since I did.' Gwen was always pleased to renew old acquaintances.

'I'll get this,' Gwen's dad offered. 'It can be my treat to say thank you for being a nice future son-in-law. And surely it's about time you called me

Frank? I can't stand this Mr Harper stuff.'

'Thank you, Frank. I'll try to remember.'

'And please introduce me as Frank to the rest of the group. I don't want to be left out as being stuffy.'

Adam laughed.

'I'm sure you could never be thought of as stuffy. After all, you're doing us a big favour with prompting.'

'I hope it will be a favour and I don't make a mess of it.'

They all walked into the hall and saw one or two of the others had already arrived. Adam took a quick look round and saw that he had arrived before the band.

Paul came in and went to speak to Frank.

'This is very good of you. We all appreciate you coming,' Paul told him.

'Thank you. I hope I don't let anyone down. I'm not entirely sure I know what to do, though.'

'You'll be fine, Dad,' Gwen reassured

him. 'I've explained it all to you and it really is fairly straightforward. Have you got a script for him, Paul?'

The director shook his head.

'I'm sorry. Crystal took it with her when she flounced off. Can he borrow one of yours?'

'He could have mine but I may forget some of my lines,' Gwen said. 'I usually like to check the next bit when I'm off stage.'

'He can have mine,' Adam offered. 'I think I know it pretty well. If not, he can always prompt me.'

They laughed.

There was sudden chaos at the back of the hall as the band arrived, bringing their instruments.

Adam went off to join them and help carry in the various pieces of equipment.

'We've brought our amplifiers which we can turn down fairly low, but it will give a better performance,' Tom told him.

'What's all this?' Mrs Probert asked

loudly as she entered the hall. 'I hope they're not going to spoil our play. All that loud music . . . well, it's terrible. I can't think why they've all come here. This is not the place for their sort of noise.'

'Mrs Probert, you missed the last rehearsal, I believe,' Paul pointed out. 'We agreed Adam should make enquiries about the band coming along and here they are.'

Mrs Probert tutted.

'I couldn't manage the last rehearsal. Pity, as I certainly would never have voted for this rabble to be brought in,' she complained.

'I'm sorry, Mrs Probert,' Adam replied tersely. 'Do you know who they are?'

The woman shook her head.

'No, I don't — and glad I am, too.'

'This group are called the Last Word. They are really well known in the area and very good they are, too. Unless you've heard them playing before, you're in no position to criticise.'

Mrs Probert shrugged dismissively.

'I'm entitled to my opinion, young man. I say they should never have been asked to come here.'

'I would suggest that if you don't like their sound, you leave us all right now,' Adam retorted. 'Go home, Mrs Probert. You're not wanted here.'

A faint ripple of applause came out from the rest of the cast.

'How dare you speak to me like that? Paul? Are you going to allow him to speak to me like that?' Mrs Probert demanded.

Paul took a deep breath.

'I think he has a point. I'm not sure why you're here. You don't have a role and don't help in any way. No, I think I would second his comments.'

The older lady was shocked.

'Well, really. You should all be ashamed of yourselves. I've been a member of this group since it first started. I demand an apology from this young man and I will not go home. Why should I?'

'Oh, for goodness' sake,' Paul snapped, exhausted by the woman's constant carping. He turned to Adam. 'Could you bear to apologise to this woman so she can go home?'

'I don't see why I should.' Adam was furious and in great danger of saying something she really would object to. 'No, certainly not. There's no apology due from me, but there is from her. Shall we get on with the rehearsal?'

Jack stepped forward to speak, hoping to resolve the situation.

'Perhaps if you hear their music, you might change your mind. I've certainly heard them and in no way would I call them a rabble. They are very talented and having them on board will make a huge difference to the play,' he commented.

'In your opinion. I have my own opinion,' Mrs Probert continued. 'If you want to ruin this pathetic play even more, it's up to you. I'm just glad I'm not involved.'

'Pity she doesn't go back where she

came from,' one of the others muttered too loudly.

Mrs Probert scowled. She swung round to glare at the rest of the group.

'You'll all miss me when I'm not here!' she almost shouted. 'Who will do front of house? Answer me that one. You won't have nearly the same amount of ticket sales. In fact, the whole thing will probably flop.'

'How many tickets have you ever sold?' Sally asked. 'Not many, in my recollection.'

'Nonsense, girl. I always sell large numbers. How would you know anyway?'

'Now then, ladies,' Paul put in, ever the peacemaker, 'let us get on with the rehearsal. We've wasted enough time. Mrs Probert, I would suggest you leave us now and perhaps come back at some point when you've regained your stability.'

'Are you calling me unstable? How dare you.' She was turning practically purple.

Paul closed his eyes, as if he was praying for her to simply disappear.

'If the cap fits,' came a mutter from the group.

Mrs Probert swung round again, ready to shout again, but instead she fell down in some sort of dead faint.

'Oh!' Adam cried.

The group rushed forward, panicking, but Mrs Probert was already coming round and she sat up, looking slightly bemused.

'Are you OK, Mrs Probert?' Gwen asked.

'Don't be ridiculous, girl. I must have been so disturbed by all your rudeness, I fainted. Help me up. I'm going now and good riddance to you all and the wretched pantomime, or whatever you call it.' She gave a sniff and walked out of the hall slightly unsteadily.

'Do you think someone should go with her?' Gwen asked.

'I doubt she'd let anyone,' Adam replied. 'She only lives round the corner. I'm sure she'll be all right. She's got a husband at home, poor old thing.'

'That's unusually sympathetic of you, Adam.'

'I was thinking of her husband as a poor old thing actually,' he replied guiltily. 'Now, can we please get on?'

10

A Song in His Heart

The entire cast gave a sigh of relief as Mrs Probert left the hall. They had wasted the best part of half an hour with all the fuss. It was especially difficult with the band sitting there waiting for things to get underway.

'OK, we'll go from the beginning,' Paul announced. 'Everyone for the first scene on stage, please.'

Adam went over to the band and chatted in a whisper to them.

'I thought we could do a kind of overture while the audience are settling,' he explained. 'It doesn't really matter what, but something with just sound and no vocals. I'll keep coming to you to explain what we want as we go along.'

They wound on through the various

scenes, with Adam leaping off the stage and speaking to the band in between.

'Can we try one of the numbers for the next scene? Maybe the one we planned on Saturday? I can do the main vocals and you can do the backing,' he asked.

'Sure,' Tom agreed. 'It makes us bringing all the gear worthwhile.'

'I'm sorry. Things haven't worked out as I planned due to that wretched woman,' Adam complained. 'I bet you anything she'll be round here again very soon. Talk about thick-skinned.

'Right,' he continued. 'Be ready for the scene when I meet Cindy and we start to fall in love. I'll give you a signal.'

It all worked beautifully. Adam had a good singing voice and the number went down well. The cast all applauded him after the number and suggested more singing should be included.

Paul smiled happily for the first time that evening. They continued with the rehearsal and he made some notes about including more songs.

It was almost half past ten by the time they reached the end of the play.

'Thank you so much, everyone,' Paul said to the group. 'I'm not going to give you heaps of notes this time. It's been a mixed sort of evening, what with outbursts from one member and trying to fit in music. Can we have another rehearsal tomorrow for just music?'

'I'm sorry, I'm on duty,' Gwen admitted. 'I won't finish till after nine so you'll have to count me out. Mind you, with a voice like mine, that should be a relief to everyone.'

Several of the others were equally negative about their voices.

'We can't really sing,' Sally said. 'I've got a voice like a foghorn.'

'You'll be fine. The band will provide the main sound and you can simply dance around.'

'Hang on,' James said. 'We have a number where someone can almost

155

speak their lines. We sing the song and they pop in with the spoken lines. It's sure to work.'

Paul nodded thoughtfully.

'Let's look at it tomorrow. I need some sleep now. Thank you very much, all of you. I will see those of you who can come tomorrow.'

Gwen and Adam walked over to where Frank was putting on his coat.

'Well, Dad, how did you get on?' Gwen asked. 'You seemed reasonably happy, sitting in your corner.'

He smiled.

'I quite enjoyed it all once I got into it. You've got a good voice, Adam. I didn't realise it before.'

Adam looked embarrassed.

'Thank you. I used to be with the band but gave up a few years ago. I did enjoy singing with them again. I'll drop you home and then try to get some sleep. I feel dead on my feet.'

Once Adam had driven Gwen and her father home, he set off back to his flat. Exhausted, he went into his bedroom and flopped down on his bed. He fell asleep immediately.

★ ★ ★

Adam woke to his alarm and felt greatly refreshed. He leaped up, showered and made some toast and coffee.

Soon he was on his way to work and ready to put in a decent day. It made a change after the past day or two and all his concerns about the pantomime.

At the hall that evening, they worked well together and soon had all the musical numbers sorted. Gwen was working so the rest of them planned and rehearsed what they were going to do.

'It's amazing how easy it all seemed,' Marie said afterwards. 'I really can't sing all that well, but with the band playing and supporting, I don't think I made too bad a job of it.'

'Not at all. It sounded good,' James said. 'We might even invite you to do a guest spot with the band.'

'No! I couldn't think of anything worse,'

Marie retorted with a laugh. 'Heavens, the panto is bad enough.'

Adam's phone rang.

'Excuse me,' he said. 'It's Gwen, so I should see what she wants. I thought she was working tonight.

'Hi, darling. What's up?'

Immediately Adam could tell she was in tears.

'Oh, Adam, I can't believe it. My car's been stolen, like yours was. I'm stuck out here with no transport. Dad's out and you're the only person I could think of.'

'I'll be with you in a few minutes,' he promised. 'Where are you exactly?'

'Out at a farm beyond Penzance,' Gwen replied. 'Not far from Chysauster. It really is in the middle of nowhere. That's why I've phoned you.'

'OK. It'll take me a while. Don't worry.' Adam turned to the rest of the group. 'I'm sorry. I'll have to leave now. Someone's stolen Gwen's car and I need to fetch her.'

'Oh, dear, that's really tough. There's too much of that sort of thing going on round here.' Marie frowned. 'Yes, you go, Adam. Send our love and tell her the police will get to the bottom of it.'

'I just hope it hasn't been burned like mine was,' Adam replied. 'I hate these yobs who take whatever they want. She was in a very out of the way place. It definitely sounds more like vengeance than them wanting transport. I'd better go. Thanks very much, all of you.' He almost ran out of the hall, so anxious he was to reach his fiancée.

★　★　★

Gwen waited inside the farmhouse, having explained to her client what had happened. The old farmer tutted and grumbled about the youth of today. His bedridden wife muttered that Gwen would never come out here again and began to sob.

'Don't worry,' Gwen assured her. 'Of course I'll come again. It's just some folks who think they can get away with taking anything they fancy. I'm sure Adam will be here soon. In fact, I think I should go outside and wait for him.'

'Stay close to the gate,' the farmer urged. 'I don't want you putting yourself in any danger.'

'I'll wait in the porch and then you can settle down. I'll say goodbye and leave you now.'

Gwen went outside and the farmer locked the door behind her. She stood there in the dark night watching for lights to approach.

She stamped her feet as quietly as she could and began to feel thoroughly chilled. Perhaps she'd been foolish to stand outside but she could see the old couple needed to settle down for the night. She wondered whether to go back inside but saw lights coming from a distance away.

'Thank goodness,' she murmured.

As the lights got closer, she went out into the road to wait for him to arrive.

'Oh, Adam!' she cried when she got in the car. 'I'm so sorry to drag you out here. I'm sure it was those blokes I saw in the pub. They must have followed me out here and taken the car when I was busy inside.'

Adam hugged her.

'Are you all right?' he asked, concerned. 'It's no fun being stuck out here at this time of night.'

'I'm OK. Just a bit shaken up and angry with whoever took my car. There's all my notes and stuff in the car. What shall I do?'

'Don't worry, love. If they have got your notes, what will they do with them? Think about it.'

Gwen nodded.

'I am and I don't like it. The office will go mad. There's all sorts of confidential stuff in there — addresses of clients and everything.' Gwen was on the verge of tears.

Adam dried her tears with his sleeve.

'Please, stop worrying. There's nothing you can do about it — not tonight anyway.'

'Perhaps I should phone the office. Not that there will be anyone there, but I could leave a message on the answering machine.'

Adam shook his head.

'I think you should leave it till morning,' he suggested. 'You'll need to call the police tonight.'

'I should have called from the farm,' Gwen suddenly realised. 'I never thought about it. I was just so anxious to leave the farmer and his wife in peace.'

'I'll drive you to the police station, so you can report it right away.'

Gwen smiled.

'Trust you to get me organised. Thank you.'

★   ★   ★

It was almost ten o'clock by the time they reached the police station. They saw the desk sergeant who gave a sigh and said they were getting far too many of these sort of incidents. He noted down the details.

'It's those wretched gangs of youths who get bored with life and nick cars to give them something to do.' He was obviously a bored young man, possibly feeling aggrieved at being on late duty.

'We have our suspicions about who might have done this.' Adam was determined to have his say. 'A couple of people threatened Gwen in the pub the other night. She was in such an out of the way place, we think it might have been the same men.'

'Leave us to find the culprits, sir.'

'If you can. You haven't found anyone guilty of my car theft, yet. They burned it, too.'

The police officer looked mildly guilty.

'Sorry, sir. I may have read about that one. I'll certainly look at your crime as well as this one.'

Adam nodded.

'Well, thank you, officer. We'll leave it with you. You've got both our contact numbers and my address is also on record.'

'I'm sure we'll find whoever is guilty.'

'I hope so. Come on, Gwen. It's high time you were tucked up in bed.'

As they walked out of the police station, Gwen stopped suddenly, realising the severity of her situation.

'What on earth am I going to do? I can't manage without a car. I need a car for work. Plus there's everything I've still got to do before the wedding!'

'Perhaps the police will find your car quickly,' Adam replied. 'If it really is just a revenge attack, they'll leave it somewhere.'

'You don't really believe that, do you?' Gwen returned. 'Those blokes didn't seem to be joking when they said Crystal wasn't best pleased about losing her part in the play. They didn't actually know it was me who had taken over her role, but they could soon have discovered it. I really do feel very vulnerable.'

Adam reached out to hug her as she began to cry again.

'I'm sorry,' he said, pushing a lock of hair from her eyes. 'I do understand. I felt the same when my car was stolen. We'll go and see the police again tomorrow. I'll drop you home now and be round first thing in the morning.'

* * *

Despite feeling exhausted, neither of them slept much. Gwen was worried about her missing folders and Adam was simply furious about someone having stolen Gwen's car.

It was all too much. His own vehicle had been ruined by someone viciously taking it, and now Gwen was also being punished. Nobody could surely feel so aggrieved about losing a part in some silly drama production?

Crystal Parkinson certainly had some undesirable friends, if it really was them who were guilty.

Adam got up early and immediately called Gwen.

'I hope I didn't wake you,' he said.

'Don't think I slept much,' she replied. 'I was worrying about the folders that have gone missing — and the car, of course. Can you give me a lift to the office?'

'Of course I will,' Adam told her. 'It's not too far out of my way. I'll pick you up about half past eight. Don't worry about the folders. If they've burned the car like they did with mine, they'll have gone anyway.'

Gwen gasped.

'That's awful. All my notes and everything! I'm beginning to think this wretched play is more trouble than it's worth. I'd willingly let that stupid girl have her part back if she was any good at it.'

Adam had rarely known his fiancée to be so upset.

'I'll see you soon, love,' he told her and hung up the phone.

He hoped the police could catch the culprits sooner rather than later.

11

A Vexing Situation

Gwen's colleagues were very sympathetic. They tried to comfort her and set about trying to source copies of some of the items from the missing folders.

'I think I need to call the police,' she said. 'They might even have some news for me.'

'Please do call. I hope they have some good news.' Her boss was being particularly kind this morning, she thought.

Gwen dialled the number, but they had no news for her.

'Sorry, ma'am, but nobody has spotted it anywhere. We'll let you know as soon as we have any news. My guess is they've parked it in someone's garage or left it in some out of the way place. Speak to your insurance company and organise a hire car. I'll give you the report number to quote.' The officer did so and she wrote it down.

She hung up the phone, looking helpless.

'They told me to organise a hire car. The only people who get any benefit out of all this are the hire company,' she complained.

'There are heaps of things you can do here today,' her boss replied. 'Call your insurance and organise your car, then I'll find you something to do.'

The day seemed to drag for both Adam and Gwen. The thought of the rehearsal that evening was almost too much.

They met at his flat after work.

'We really do have to go,' Adam reasoned. 'We can't let everyone down by not turning up. The band are going to be there, too, and we really need to finalise their input.'

'The thought of actually singing is almost too much,' Gwen admitted. 'If it wasn't so near to the performance, I think I'd abandon the whole thing.'

'Come on, Gwen. You know you can't do that.'

She shook her head, looking resigned.

'Oh, don't listen to me. I just feel depressed about the car and the reason someone has stolen it. Do you really think Crystal put them up to it?'

'I wouldn't be surprised. She does know some awful types.'

'But to do that? She must be insane.'

Adam shrugged.

'Well, she's not the innocent we all took her for. I bet Geoffrey doesn't know half of what she gets up to.'

'Perhaps he does and she's just out of control,' Gwen suggested and Adam nodded.

'Shall we have something to eat?' He changed the subject. 'I can cook something before we leave for rehearsal.'

With a sigh, Gwen agreed.

★   ★   ★

An hour later, the pair arrived at the hall. Frank was already there and waiting for the rest of the group to arrive. The band had also arrived and were busy carrying their things in.

Adam went to help them while Gwen caught up with her dad.

By seven-thirty, everyone seemed to be there and ready to make a start. The band began to play the overture and they were off.

For once things went reasonably smoothly, with only Geoffrey making a meal of his part. He was actually quite good, except for the fact that he still ad-libbed most of his lines.

There were a few small hold-ups while the band worked out who was singing, but on the whole it was coming together well.

Paul spoke at the end of the rehearsal.

'Well done, everyone. Another two or three run-throughs and we'll be ready to perform.'

He mentioned one or two small

points then turned to sales of tickets.

'We need everyone to sell as many tickets as possible. If each of you could sell ten, that would give us a decent audience. Any more than ten would be a bonus.

'See you all the day after tomorrow.' He laughed. 'I've lost track of what day that is!'

'Thursday, Paul. We'll see you on Thursday.' They all laughed and went through to the bar.

'I'm going to ask Geoffrey if he knows what Crystal was doing last night,' Gwen told Adam.

'Be careful,' he warned. 'I'll come with you. I don't want you being accused of slander.'

'I was just going to ask how she is now — I'm not going to start making accusations.'

'Well, be careful.' He started to go across the room with her and was stopped by one of the band who wanted to ask him something.

Gwen went over to her target and

asked how his daughter was faring.

'She's doing all right, thanks,' Geoffrey replied. 'She's very disappointed about losing her part in this play, though. She was doing so well, too.'

'I suppose she's getting bored with staying in every night.'

'Well, perhaps so. Not that she's stayed in all the time. She has a friend who seems to call for her most nights,' he told her. 'They were at the theatre last night. Saw the ballet or something.'

'That's nice for her,' Gwen said, smiling. 'Which one did she see?'

'Oh, I don't know. 'Swan Lake' or something.'

'Well, I hope she's soon better.' She turned away and went back to Adam.

'Apparently she was at the ballet last night,' she stated.

'I bet she wasn't. She's a devious little brat. I bet she followed you with her boyfriend and saw where you were parked last night.' Adam glowered in frustration.

'I can't say anything to Geoffrey

173

anyway. He'd never believe it if we did.' Gwen grimaced. 'I think we have to leave it to the police. I think I'm going to get a lift back with Dad, if you don't mind. I feel shattered. You stay and enjoy a drink.'

'If you're sure.'

She nodded and gave him a quick kiss.

'OK. Call me if you need help.' He watched her as she left him with his friends.

James watched her go, a smile on his face.

'If you don't settle down with her soon, I might just try to steal her from under your nose,' he joked.

'You won't do that.' Adam laughed. 'No way. She's mine and staying that way.'

'Have you named a day yet?'

'That's for you to find out. Now, can we please change the subject?'

'Sure we can. But I think you have plans of some sort.' James had a broad grin on his face and Adam wondered if

Gwen had said something to him.

He shook his head and turned away.

'You ready for another pint, Dave?' Adam asked.

12

So Many Secrets

Gwen was determined to find Adam's brother, Rory. She had sent two e-mails to the two men she thought could possibly be him, but had heard nothing back. She sat staring at her screen, wondering what to try next.

Her father had suggested one of the social media sites, but she felt unwilling to go down that route. She put the name into the search engine again and waited. She would contact one of the men she had thought unlikely to be Rory, just in case.

One of the men had a website which suggested he was a sculptor. Somehow, she didn't think he was the right person, but she decided to contact him anyway. She pressed the 'Contact me' button and wrote him a message.

'Do you have a brother called Adam? If you do, please contact me.'

Adam had never mentioned that Rory had anything at all to do with sculpture, but as he admitted himself, he hadn't known his brother since he went into the Army. But surely they must have talked when their parents died?

Gwen found the whole thing somewhat bizarre. She couldn't imagine having a brother and losing all contact with him. It looked an interesting connection if indeed this sculptor was her brother-in-law to be.

She looked around the website for a picture of the man, but there was nothing. She kept checking during the day, but no message came back. Perhaps he didn't look at his site all that often. And, of course, he might not be the right person, anyway.

⋆　⋆　⋆

The next couple of days were busy with work and rehearsals. The pantomime, as it was now, was moving on well. The new lines had all been incorporated and the music had been fitted in well.

Her scene with Paul had been kept under wraps so far, and so had Gwen and Adam's real secret wedding. She was getting excited thinking about it and the only person she could talk about it with was her dad.

He listened patiently, but he still missed his wife who would have revelled in the planning of it all.

Gwen had told the wardrobe mistress that she would bring her own dress for the wedding on the last night, without admitting anything. The other nights she was wearing the traditional wedding dress that had previously been planned.

She was looking forward to wearing her own dress and wondered how she would get it there without anyone seeing. She wanted it to be a surprise to everyone. Lots of their friends would be in the audience and were going to be invited to stay on after the performance.

Gwen remembered she needed to organise the time the local baker should have the extra food ready. She pulled out her lists again and wrote everything down. There was so much to do.

Then she stopped. There really wasn't much to do at all. This was exactly why they'd organised such a simple wedding.

All she needed now was a reply from Rory, whoever and wherever he was. Having him there as a witness would be such a bonus. He might even have a wife and family.

She quickly powered up her laptop and looked to see if he had replied. Her heart leaped as she saw a response.

She opened his message and looked at it excitedly.

'Sorry, it's not me. No brothers at all. However, you might try this other Rory Jerrold's e-mail address. I think he may be the one you're looking for. He once contacted me, having the same name.'

He listed the e-mail address, which sounded French.

Gwen felt somewhat deflated and puzzled, but did send a thank-you message. Who on earth was this new contact she'd been sent? Very strange.

She composed a new message saying pretty much what she had said before and pressed send.

This time it took over a day to get a response.

'Hi, there. I do have a brother called Adam. Why do you want to know?'

Full of excitement, Gwen sent another message immediately.

'I'm his fiancée. We're getting married soon and it would be wonderful if you could be there with us. Where do you live? Do you have a wife and family? Gwen.'

She sat waiting, staring at her screen. He'd only just sent the message, and unless he'd turned his machine off right away, he should have seen her message quickly. She waited for another half hour but no message came.

Perhaps it had been a shock to him to get the message and he needed to think about it for a while. She left her laptop and went to get on with some tasks.

It was over an hour later before she received anything.

'Hello, Gwen. I'm still getting over the shock. I've heard nothing from Adam since our parents' funeral. Now I hear he's getting married! I'm living in northern France at present with a lovely lady who is a photographer. I help her, but since I left the Army, I haven't had a proper job. I don't really like to admit it but I suffer from a stress disorder. Most of my inheritance was spent on medical help, though I did put some of it into a home for me and Simone. Things are now looking back to normal and I shall be looking for a permanent job fairly soon. So, when are you getting married and where do you live? I'm not sure I'll be able to come but I'd like to know the details. Sincerely, Rory Jerrold.'

Gwen sat down again and thought about Adam's brother. It was awful that he'd suffered after leaving the Army.

She had no idea about the sums of money involved in the will of their parents, but if Adam had bought a flat and was thinking of buying a house, it must have been quite a considerable amount.

To think Rory had been forced to spend so much on rehabilitation was a terrible situation. She shuddered. At least he had managed to make some sort of life since then.

She sat at the machine to reply, wondering what Adam might have said.

She began to type.

'Hi, Rory, Great to hear from you. I'm sorry to hear you've suffered, but I am glad to hear you're feeling better. Our wedding is very secret with only my father knowing about the date. We're in a play together and end up getting married in the story. We are planning to announce that we are really married on the last night.

'We are getting married in the morning of the last day, which is a week on Saturday. I know it's rather short notice for you, but we'd be so thrilled to have you with us, and Simone, of course. Adam doesn't know I've been looking for you. I won't tell him about finding you unless you say you definitely won't be coming. I really look forward to meeting you some day. Gwen.'

She hesitated about signing her name. Should she put 'with love' or 'sincerely', or just leave it at 'Gwen'? She decided on the latter and pressed send. She sat back and thought about what she had done.

Adam had never said he didn't get on with his brother and she hoped he'd be pleased with her efforts and not be angry with her. Mind you, she'd only learned he even had a brother fairly recently.

She told her father about her activities when she saw him that evening.

'I hope what you've done is for the best,' was his only comment.

'I'm not sure about his financial

situation,' Gwen told him. 'I could buy them tickets to come over, but it might hurt his feelings. What do you think?'

Frank shook his head.

'Leave it well alone. I don't think that's a good idea at all.'

'You're probably right. I'll wait to see what he says. I'm so thrilled to have found him.'

'You've done very well, love.'

★   ★   ★

It was hard to keep her secret to herself that evening. When she saw Adam again at the next rehearsal she nearly told him, but knew she shouldn't say anything till closer to the time of their wedding.

'Only a week tomorrow,' she said excitedly to him. 'I can't really believe it, can you?'

'I'm looking forward to having you all to myself. Technical rehearsal Monday, dress rehearsal Tuesday, and then Wednesday is free for any further rehearsal deemed necessary. Thursday and Friday we're on and then it's Saturday!'

'There won't be much time to get nervous, will there?' She smiled and Adam nodded.

'We haven't asked anyone to be our witnesses yet, though. Do you have anyone in mind?' he asked.

'I've had one idea, but we'll have to wait and see,' Gwen replied mysteriously.

'Who? Who are you thinking about?'

'Leave it for now. I'll come up with someone very soon.'

'You're being rather mysterious, Gwen. OK, I'll leave it to you. But if you fail, I won't marry you. Just you wait and see if I don't.'

Gwen laughed.

'Oh, woe is me! What shall I do if I'm jilted at the altar?' she teased.

He grinned at her and drew her into his arms.

'There's no way I'd miss out on marrying you. Even if I have to drag someone off the street to be a witness.'

She grinned back at him and kept very quiet. If his brother could come over, it would be amazing. If not, she would ask someone from her work. Several of her colleagues were coming to the show on Saturday so it wouldn't be too long a time for them to keep it secret.

'OK, everyone,' Paul's voice cut in. 'I'll see you on Monday for the technical. It'll be a long one so be prepared for that. Gwen, could you spare an hour or so on Sunday? I'd like to go through our spot once more before everyone sees it.'

'You've kept it very secret and we're all bursting with curiosity,' Marie told them eagerly.

'Yes,' Sally agreed. 'You're out to steal the limelight.'

'Oh, it isn't that good.' Gwen laughed. 'You'll like it all right, but it's very short. It's hardly going to steal any limelight from anyone.'

'Even I've not seen it,' Adam announced grumpily. 'They're really keeping it secret.'

'All right, all right. Let's not get carried away. See you all on Monday.' Paul strode off.

⋆　⋆　⋆

Adam found it rather difficult to concentrate on his work on Monday. The day seemed to crawl by until it was finally time to leave.

He told his boss that he'd work from home the next day and it was agreed. That way he'd be available to answer the phone or do anything else that was needed.

He might even go and order his new car, but that might be pushing it a bit. He'd scarcely decided what model he wanted.

He'd leave it till next week, he decided. Now it was time he was getting ready for the rehearsal.

He called Gwen and she said she was going to the hall, with her father.

'OK. See you there soon. Bye, love.'

Paul was right when he said it would be a slow rehearsal. They kept stopping to sort out lights, operated by two members who always came in to do them.

They were also hampered by Mrs Probert's arrival soon after they started. She was furious that they'd almost sold all the tickets to the performances and had also organised two people to take the tickets and serve coffee at half time.

'Well, really!' she burst out. 'You have ignored the many years of service I've given to you voluntarily. I have never complained about standing at the door taking tickets and pouring coffee in the interval.'

'Well, we're organised for this year,' Paul's wife told her, moving her away from the stage so the actors could get on with their rehearsal. She was a very tactful lady.

Gwen was ready to do the so-called transformation scene with Paul. There was a buzz around the members and everyone fell silent as Cindy sat by the fire, looking sad at being left behind when her sisters had gone to the disco.

The door burst open and in walked Gok, — Paul dressed as Gok Wan. He looked brilliant and, as he finally transformed Cindy into the best dressed girl for the disco, the band added to their performance with a huge clash of cymbals as she stepped out in her finery.

The whole cast erupted into a burst of applause together with whistles and cheers.

Still in character, Gok did a sweeping bow as he sent Cindy off to the disco. The curtains swept across and soon they were all chatting about Paul's performance.

There was a long hold-up as the scenery became difficult to wind up from the kitchen scene to the disco. The band chimed in with one of their old numbers and Adam came through and joined in with them.

The rest of the cast who weren't occupied on stage began to dance around. The scenery was finally changed and Paul called them all on stage.

The band played a couple of disco numbers as Cindy met her man and they slowed into a cheek to cheek dance. He sang to her and she joined in and they wandered off the stage.

'You were brilliant, Gwen. Well done,' Adam said as they waited in the wings. 'I must say, I quite like you in that little number. You could wear that for the party after the show.'

She laughed.

'Paul made it very easy,' she replied with a smile. 'He was good, though, wasn't he?'

Adam nodded as Paul called the cast back to continue the show.

By eleven o'clock, they had finished. Paul stood up and congratulated everyone on their patience.

'I said it would be a long rehearsal and it certainly has been. You've all done very well,' Paul announced. 'Tomorrow we have the final dress rehearsal. We'll get the scenery sorted before tomorrow night, though I must say, I loved what the band did, and Adam, you should go and play with them. It worked really well and would keep the audience involved during the break. Well done, everyone. No prompts tomorrow.'

Marie stepped forward.

'Paul, we must all congratulate you on your performance. It was wonderful. I'm still giggling when I think of it.' She spoke on behalf of several of the others and they all joined in with their applause.

'Well, thank you. Part of it was Gwen's suggestion and she deserves your congratulations, too.'

'Yes, well done, Gwen,' Marie said with a smile. 'I think it's made the panto into something special.'

'See you tomorrow at six thirty, please!' Paul called out.

The chatter died away as everyone left. Gwen went home with her father and Adam went back to his flat, where he almost fell into bed, feeling exhausted.

* * *

At six thirty the following evening, people were starting to arrive at the hall in a buzz of excitement. There were to be a few people watching the performance that evening so it did feel like the real thing.

The roller that wound up the scenery had been fixed and the stage curtains were closed. They began to get into their costumes and two ladies were on hand to do the make-up.

Paul gave them a pep talk, saying he'd get changed when the action was taking place.

'Good luck, everyone. Go for it.'

Geoffrey arrived half an hour later, bringing Crystal with him.

'I knew you'd all be pleased to see our little star. She's had the plaster replaced. What do you think?' A couple of the cast turned round to look at the new arrival and nodded. 'Say hello to everyone, Crystal. I'm sure they're all pleased to see you.'

'Hello, everyone,' she said in a totally bored way.

'Hi, there. Glad to know you're better. Are you going to watch us tonight?' Paul asked.

'I suppose I'll have to. I have no other way to get home again till Dad's ready to leave. Can I stay in here, Dad?'

'Well, I suppose there's no harm in it,' her father replied. 'Any objections?'

'It would be very boring for her,' Adam spoke out. 'Even more boring than watching the performance.'

'You can stay till it's nearly time for us to perform,' her father told her.

She gave a shrug.

'I really don't know why you insisted I came. I don't think anyone's pleased to see me.'

Geoffrey looked around the room.

'Of course they are, my darling. Everyone's really pleased to see you're looking so much better.' One or two of them mumbled something which he took to mean they agreed. 'Now, I must transfer into a bumbling idiot of a bailiff. See you in a moment.'

He breezed off to his changing room, leaving his daughter sitting there.

She glanced at Gwen and scowled at her.

'I hope you forget all your stupid lines. Have you found your car yet?'

'What do you know about my car?' Gwen snapped.

'Wouldn't you like to know?'

'Of course I would. If it was your scum of a boyfriend who stole it, he should be ashamed of himself. I suppose he's burned it like he did Adam's.'

Crystal laughed.

'Of course he hasn't. He may have been a bit drunk when he took Adam's, but he was down to earth when he took yours. Mind you, I was pretty far gone that night.' She gave a giggle. 'It's tucked away somewhere you'll never find it.'

Her blue eyes were bright and she looked slightly crazed.

'I hope you realise it wasn't my car?' Gwen told her. 'It belongs to the care agency I work for. The ones who might have helped you, in fact.'

Crystal didn't look bothered.

'Well, I hope it's inconvenienced you a lot. That was our aim. To make your life so difficult you'd forget your lines and wreck this rubbish play. Hasn't it made your work rather difficult?' She then laughed.

'So you admit you had something to do with taking it?' Gwen wasn't completely surprised.

'Oh, now how on earth could I do that with my poor broken leg?'

'You really are the pits.' Gwen shook her head as Geoffrey came back into the room.

'All right, darling? Gwen been entertaining you all right?'

The girl smiled sweetly at her father.

'Oh, yes. She's full of entertainment.'

Gwen walked away from her, telling

Adam she'd like to throttle the girl.

'Calm down, love. We suspected it was her, but it's not the time even to think about it. Come on now — get ready for your starring role,' he encouraged her.

'Overture and beginners, please!' came the call.

It was time to begin.

13

Bursting With Excitement

At ten o'clock, Paul stood on the stage with the entire cast around him.

'Congratulations, everyone. You did a splendid job. I have one or two notes for you but nothing major. Sally and Marie, I'd like you to move more to the middle of the stage when you challenge your father.'

He continued to pass on small details to some of the cast, until he finally ran out.

He turned as a loud sigh came from the auditorium. Crystal was still sitting on her front row seat, looking very bored.

'I'm sorry? Did you want to make a contribution, Crystal?' he asked.

'I have nothing to say. A totally boring and wasted evening. Can't think why I was persuaded to come with my dad.'

'Not as exciting as drinking alcohol and stealing innocent people's cars, I suppose,' an infuriated Gwen burst out, allowing her temper to get the better of her.

'How dare you!' Geoffrey stormed. 'Take that back immediately. My daughter would never touch alcohol, much less steal cars.'

'Is that right?' Gwen turned to Crystal. 'You should tell him what you told me before the play started.'

'I don't know what you mean. Can we go now, please, Daddy? I don't like being accused of things I never did.' She seemed so sickly sweet, Gwen was totally disgusted.

'Of course we can, darling. I'll speak to you tomorrow, Gwen. How dare you go around trying to ruin someone's reputation like that?' He put his arm around his daughter and led her out of the hall.

Gwen felt close to tears and moved

away from the rest of the group.

Adam went over to her and put his arms round her. He knew exactly how she was feeling and really wanted to help her.

'She virtually admitted it was her — or rather her boyfriend. They were drunk when they took your car. She said mine was tucked away somewhere I'd never find it. I said it wasn't mine and belonged to work.'

'But it is yours, isn't it?'

Gwen nodded tearfully.

'Well, yes, but I wanted to make her sweat a bit. I'm just feeling angry that nobody else heard her admission and we can't prove anything. She looks so innocent with her big blue eyes. Her father will never believe it.'

'Come on. Let's go and have a glass of wine. Only four more days of freedom,' he whispered.

'I can't wait.' She smiled at him as they went through to the bar.

★ ★ ★

Despite the lateness of the hour, Gwen went to look at her e-mails when she got home. To her great delight, there was a message from Rory.

'Hi, Gwen. I think you'll be pleased to know that Simone and I have decided we will come over for your wedding. Is there somewhere we can stay? We'll be in Cornwall on Friday, ready for your wedding on the Saturday. We'll bring our car over on the ferry. I look forward to meeting you and to seeing Adam again. Rory.'

'Dad! Where are you?' Gwen shouted.

'I'm in bed. What's wrong?'

Gwen entered his room and burst into tears.

'Hey, come here. What's wrong?'

'Nothing. Everything's wonderful. Rory is coming over for the wedding. He and Simone are coming on the ferry and will be here on Friday. You won't mind if I say they can stay here, will you?'

'Of course not, love, but won't they

want to be with Adam?'

'Well, maybe — but he's only got one bedroom. Anyway, we can sort all that later. Oh, I'm so thrilled. I know Adam will be, too.'

'Well, I hope so, love. I think he might be a bit shocked. When will you tell him?'

'I suppose it should be before Rory actually arrives. Perhaps I need to say something tomorrow. What do you think?'

Frank looked thoughtful.

'I think I'd tell him tomorrow. He might need to get over the shock. You've got a performance on Thursday and then his brother will be here the next day. Yes, I think you need to tell him tomorrow.'

Gwen nodded.

'I'll tell him tomorrow evening. We're supposed to be meeting to organise drinks for the party. We've put in a provisional order at the bar but we need to finalise it. I'll tell him then.'

Frank smiled.

'You've done really well, love,' he told her. 'Tell them they are welcome to stay here.'

'Great. I'll e-mail them right away. They'll get it in the morning and make their plans.'

She ran downstairs again and e-mailed them, saying how thrilled she was that they were coming. She included a map showing where she lived and told them they were welcome to stay at her home.

She pressed send and sat smiling. It was all going to be perfect.

★　★　★

Adam was working the next day and then had organised his holiday. He felt the need to take a few days off, particularly after the wedding and party. He meant to look for a hotel or somewhere they could go and stay for a couple of nights. They were planning a proper honeymoon later when the weather improved.

They could discuss it when Gwen came round that evening. What was it they were planning to talk about? Then he remembered. It was the wine for the party. Somehow, he had to order it from the bar without arousing suspicions as to the reasons behind an increase.

They both worked hard to clear everything they'd been doing and Gwen went home from work soon after four. It felt a bit odd to her going back home without any sort of send off. The girls she worked with usually had a celebration when someone was getting married.

Adam finally finished his own work slightly later than six and went back to his flat. He'd planned to cook something special for supper but it would have to be something simple after all.

He called Gwen when he arrived home.

'Are you coming round soon? I haven't actually bought anything for supper yet. We could go to the pub if you like.'

'It's OK,' Gwen replied. 'I'll bring some steak and we can do a salad with it.'

She was nearly bursting with excitement by the time she arrived at Adam's flat. She kissed him when she arrived and he seemed surprised by her enthusiasm.

'What was that in aid of?' He laughed.

'Nothing. I'm just pleased to see you and I'm on holiday. We've got a whole week off work.'

'You're a bit happier than you were last night,' he pointed out. 'Last night you were spitting feathers because you couldn't prove Crystal was behind our car thefts.'

'Yes, but let's not think about her. I've actually got some news. Pour some wine and I'll tell you.'

He took some glasses out of the cupboard and poured wine, as instructed.

'Sit down,' Gwen told him and he did so, looking slightly puzzled. 'It's about your brother. Rory. I've found him and he's coming over to the wedding.'

Adam was shocked.

'What? I don't understand.'

Gwen began to explain.

'He lives in France with someone called Simone. They're coming over on Friday and will be here for the wedding. They can act as our witnesses. What do you think of that?' She looked at him, eager for his reaction.

Adam sat quietly for several minutes, allowing the news to sink in.

'I did do the right thing in finding him, didn't I?' she asked nervously.

'I . . . I don't know. Yes, of course you did. But it's such a shock. How on earth did you find him?' Adam said finally.

'Various searches and then someone sent me his e-mail address,' Gwen explained.

'So when did you actually find Rory?'

'A couple of days ago. I only got his message last night when I got home. He said they're coming over by ferry and bringing their car so they can be independent. I've said they can stay at our place. You have only one bedroom anyway.'

Adam smiled.

'Gwen Harper, you are full of surprises,' he said. 'You've actually traced my long lost brother and organised him to come to our wedding? You really are a miracle worker. Now, tell me his address and we'll contact him right away.'

'Shouldn't we have dinner first?' Gwen asked. 'I'm starving. Another half an hour won't make any difference.'

'Fair enough. Is he on Skype? I want to know what he looks like now.' Adam was starting to get used to the idea.

'I'll heat the grill. I don't know if he's on Skype. I'll give you his e-mail address in a while. Now, you prepare some salad and I'll do the steak. There's some bread in my bag, too. Could you slice some of that, please?'

'What did he say?' Adam persisted.

Gwen laughed at Adam's new-found eagerness.

'He said he'd left the Army and, well, he suffered what I take to be PTSD . . . Post Traumatic Stress Disorder. He said he'd spent most of the money your parents left to him on helping him cope with that.'

Adam nodded.

'Did he say how he met Simone?' he said. 'Why does he live in France?'

Gwen shrugged.

'No, and I don't know. We can ask him everything when he's here. Now, are you going to put that salad together or have I got to do that as well?'

Eventually they sat down to their meal with Adam plaguing Gwen with questions. She felt she had told him word for word everything she knew about his brother, his partner and the person who had put them in touch.

As soon as they had both finished eating, Adam switched on his computer and typed in the e-mail address Gwen had given him.

'It's a strange address,' he said. 'I'm not sure what to say now.'

Gwen was thoughtful.

'What about 'Hello, Rory. This feels so strange. I'm so pleased to be in touch with you again and delighted you're coming over. Do you know what time you'll arrive in Cornwall? Then I'd send your love and leave it at that.'

He nodded.

After he had sent it, he sat staring at the screen, as if waiting for a reply.

'He's possibly gone out for the evening,' Gwen said sensibly. 'He may not reply tonight. Let's work out what we need for Saturday night. Are we just offering beer and wine?'

'I think so.' Adam nodded. 'They are going to do the bar anyway. Do you think he's got the message yet?'

'Oh, Adam, really! Can we get back to this order? We don't want to run out, do we? There are twenty-six of us involved in the play plus relatives, so that makes fifty-two. I'm planning to invite ten from work, and then there are other hangers on. How many have you invited?'

'I don't know. About ten as well. That's seventy-two at least. Quite a lot, isn't it?'

'It would have been much more if it was a proper wedding,' she pointed out.

'Proper wedding? I knew it! You don't think it is a proper wedding, do you?'

Gwen laughed.

'Of course I do!' she assured Adam. 'I was just using a sort of shorthand. It will be a proper wedding and a lovely occasion.'

Adam looked once more at the computer.

'He still hasn't answered. Do you think he's changed his mind?' he asked.

'No, Adam, I don't. He doesn't sit looking at his computer screen all the time. So how many bottles should we order? And how many red or white?'

'Ask the barman. He'll suggest how many. Tell him how many people will be there and leave it to him.' He paused. 'I'm going to send Rory another e-mail. Perhaps you got the address wrong.'

'If you don't leave it alone, I'm

going home,' Gwen warned him good-naturedly. 'He will reply, but who knows when? He might not have his computer switched on at all.'

'Actually, they are an hour ahead of us, aren't they?' Adam checked his watch. 'That means it must be almost ten o'clock there. Perhaps they're having an early night. I'll get a reply in the morning.'

They spent the rest of the evening talking about their plans and Gwen arranged to go shopping the next morning to ensure she had food in to feed the visitors.

'I'd better stock up for you, too, in case they want to come here,' she told him.

'I'm sure they will. They could stay here and I can sleep on the couch.'

Adam chose that moment to look at his computer again and saw that there was a message there.

He opened it quickly and began to read.

'Hi, little bro! It seems strange to be

communicating like this after all these years. I'm sorry we lost touch but now we've found each other, it won't happen again. We're so looking forward to coming over to see you getting married and renew old relationships. I can't imagine what you even look like now or what you've done with your life. Gwen is obviously very caring and it looks as if you've found a good one there. I shall see you the day after tomorrow. We're travelling on the overnight ferry so will be in Cornwall by early afternoon. Rory.'

Adam sat quietly for a few moments, digesting the message. Gwen saw he had tears in his eyes but said nothing. She knew he needed a little peace and time to digest hearing from his brother again.

She collected the dinner plates and took them through to the kitchen. She soon washed them up and dried them.

Adam was very tidy for a bachelor living on his own, and he had some nice things. Admittedly, some of it was her own choice, but she knew she would be very happy living here.

She went back into the other room and stood looking over his shoulder.

He put his hand up to touch hers.

'I don't know how to thank you for finding Rory. I didn't realise how important he was to me until I saw his name on a message. Thank you so much for all your efforts. 'He rose from his seat and kissed her tenderly. 'I can't wait for Saturday, but now it's all been made even more perfect by you. The day after tomorrow I'll see my brother again and it's all down to you. Thank you.'

Gwen smiled.

'Hush or you'll set me off crying. I'm just so happy it worked out. I must admit, I was giving up all hope of finding him until the sculptor sent his message.' She checked the time. 'I'd better go now. I borrowed Dad's car as I haven't hired one for me yet.'

'What will you do tomorrow?' Adam asked. 'I mean, you're planning a big shop and all sorts of other stuff so you'll need a car.'

'I can drop Dad at his work and use his car all day,' she replied. 'As long as I pick him up at the end of his day.'

'I could come with you,' Adam suggested. 'Pick you up first thing. There isn't much I've got to do apart from see the barman, and I can do that in the evening.'

'Well, if you're sure. Thanks.'

They parted on his doorstep and he watched as she drove away.

'Not long now,' he murmured.

14

First Night Jitters

The day passed quickly and soon it was time to go to the hall for their first night.

There was a distinct buzz among the entire cast and helpers as they all got into their clothes.

The band arrived and set up their speakers and instruments and then retired to the bar, where Adam was attempting to put in his order for extra wine for their Saturday after-show party.

'Adam. What are you having to drink?' James asked.

'I'm not drinking at the moment. I'm too busy, and besides, a drunken lead male wouldn't be good.' He laughed.

'We're just having a half pint so please don't worry about us.'

'As if!' He laughed again. 'See you later.'

'Good luck. Break a leg — or whatever it is they say.'

Adam went backstage and joined in the general chat and soon it was time for curtain up.

The band played their overture and they were off.

The play was just getting going when Mrs Probert entered the hall and went straight to the front to look for a place to sit. There was nowhere available and she made such a fuss that Marie completely forgot her lines and needed to be prompted.

The woman went to the back of the hall, grumbling all the way and disturbing both audience and players. They all cursed her thoughtlessness, but the pantomime progressed until it was Geoffrey's turn to come on.

At first the audience laughed at his bumbling, assuming it was part of his role. He then began a speech that came much later in the play and would have cut out a lot of action.

Adam stepped into the breech and asked him a question that brought him back to the correct place. He saw Frank looking desperate in the wings and he gave him a thumbs-up sign.

After that, it all went smoothly, including Adam's song with the band. Paul's Fairy Gok Mother went down a storm and the audience applauded him as he went off.

'Well done, everyone. And Adam, well done for getting Geoffrey back on course,' Paul said once the cast were off stage.

'What do you mean? I never forgot anything,' the man protested.

'No, of course you didn't,' Paul agreed. 'But you went on so far ahead we'd have missed loads of action. Adam did very well to get you back on course.'

Goeffrey frowned.

'I don't know what you're talking about,' he huffed. 'Anyway, I must get back to see my daughter's all right. She was very upset the other night. Being accused of all that nonsense!'

Gwen stood back, biting her tongue. She was determined not to start an argument.

Adam put his arm round her and gave her a squeeze.

'What was all that about?' Sally asked. 'I could see something was up the other day.'

Gwen began to explain.

'Crystal admitted she was involved in stealing my car, yet she manages to fool her father that she's innocent. In fact, I think she looked pretty drunk when she was sitting here the other day.'

'Good heavens!' Sally explained. 'I wondered what was wrong with her. She looked well out of it when she was watching the performance.'

'I wish you'd heard what she said to me,' Gwen went on. 'No-one would believe me. Anyway, I'd better go home and get some rest. I have a busy day tomorrow.'

'Doing anything special?' Sally asked.

'Lots to do. Cooking and stuff. You know what it's like.'

Adam drove her home.

'What can I do to help tomorrow?' he asked.

'Nothing really. I sent Rory and Simone instructions on how to get to our place, so come round when you like. I was planning a meal for them when they arrive.'

'You're very organised, my love.' He squeezed her hand. 'I'll come round in the morning and give you a hand. I can't wait. I bet I don't sleep tonight.'

'You'll be fine. That's the first night over and done with,' Gwen reminded him. 'What more is there to worry about?'

★   ★   ★

Despite his predictions, Adam fell asleep within minutes of his head hitting his pillow.

He woke around five-thirty and lay

there, wondering where Rory and Simone were. He didn't think they'd have slept very well and would probably need to go to bed early that night.

He wanted them to be bright-eyed and bushy-tailed the next day, ready for their wedding. He could scarcely believe it would be happening so soon.

He knew he needed to get some more sleep, but his mind was far too active. He finally gave up and rose at half past six.

He tidied around the flat and put clean sheets on his bed, just in case Rory and Simone wanted to stay at his place.

He also decided to wear his new suit for the wedding scene in the play, so he'd match his bride. He occupied himself, mooching around till nine o'clock and then decided to go to Gwen's house.

'Goodness, you're early,' Gwen said as he came in.

'Sorry. I was awake so I got up and I've done everything I could. I thought

I'd come and see if there's anything I could do for you?'

'I can see I need to keep you busy with something. Do you want to vacuum the living-room? That should keep you busy for a while.'

'Anything to help.' He grinned. 'Has your dad gone to work?'

'There was no point in him staying around,' Gwen pointed out. 'We're here to welcome your brother.'

'Of course. This time tomorrow . . . Are you nervous?' Adam asked and Gwen shook her head.

'Not at all. I think I'm too busy to be nervous. I can't be bothered with all the make-up stuff and hairdressers. I shall wash my hair in the morning and that will be it. I'm leaving it loose.'

'I'm sure you'll look lovely. Now, where's the vacuum cleaner?'

The two of them worked for a while until Gwen called him into the kitchen for a coffee. They were halfway through drinking it when she noticed a car stopping outside.

'Is that them?' she asked.

Adam leaped up and rushed to the door. The driver came out and stood for a moment, then he moved towards Adam and put his arms round him.

'Hello, little brother. It's so good to see you.'

'And you!' Adam exclaimed. 'You've lost weight since I last saw you.'

'It was about ten years ago, wasn't it?' Rory turned to his passenger. 'Come and meet my brother, Simone. This is Adam.'

'Hello,' the dark-haired woman said with a strong French accent as she got out of the car. 'I am so pleased to meet you.'

'Welcome to England, and especially to Cornwall. Come on in and meet Gwen,' Adam urged. 'We're just having coffee. I expect you'd like some?'

Simone smiled as they entered the house.

'That would be wonderful. Hello, Gwen. I am so pleased to meet you. I also need to use your facilities, please.'

Her voice was almost musical sounding.

'Let me show you the way.' The two of them went upstairs and were heard chatting away.

'I'll put the kettle on. Did you have a good crossing?' Adam asked.

Rory shrugged.

'A bit rough, but not too bad. I take it this is Gwen's house?'

Adam nodded.

'Well, her father's. Her mother died years ago.'

'Oh, that's sad. We were lucky with our parents really. They were with us for most of our lives while we were growing. Gwen must have missed having a mother when preparing for her wedding.'

'I suppose so,' Adam replied. 'We've made it as simple as possible so she doesn't have the huge fuss that some people have. She'd really miss having a mum in attendance if it were a big wedding. I think we're doing the right thing, and having you here as witnesses will make so much difference to us both.

'Anyway, tell me about Simone,' he continued. 'And you living in France — how did that come about?'

'When I left the Army I went travelling around Europe. I ended up in France and met Simone. I was in a bit of a state actually. Post Traumatic Stress Disorder. I'm sure you've heard of it?'

'Yes, of course. I'm so sorry.'

'Well . . . I met Simone at the perfect time. She took me in and helped me enormously. She's a photographer, you know,' Rory explained.

'I think Gwen told me that.'

'I was able to help her and that helped me to come to terms with what had happened to me,' he went on. 'I'm pretty much as good as new now. But enough about me. I need to know about you and Gwen. What have you done with your life?'

Adam considered where to begin.

'I work in IT,' he started. 'A company in Penzance. Gwen's a carer, but she does more than that. She does a lot of the organising for the company. I bought a small flat with my share of our parents' money and kept some back for later. We'll buy a bigger house soon.'

Rory nodded, smiling.

'It sounds like you've got your life sorted. I'm not actually sure what happened to my share of our parents' money. I put some of it in some sort of investment pack and basically forgot about it.'

'You may be worth a fortune then,' Adam teased. 'Here, drink your coffee before it goes cold. I'll give the girls a call.'

They all chatted for the rest of the morning and it was soon time to think about eating. Gwen had prepared a casserole and heated it up.

'Goodness, we're not used to eating a meal at lunchtime. It's lovely, though,' Simone said.

'You speak excellent English,' Adam told her. 'Where did you learn?'

'I lived in London for a while, but I

had already learned the basics,' she replied. 'I managed to pick up on some slang, too. I won't embarrass you by saying anything now.'

'It sounds pretty good to me. I'd like to see some of your pictures, too. Do you have any with you?' Adam asked.

'I may have a few. I do have my cameras, and there are some shots on those. I was hoping to take some of your wedding, if that's all right?' Simone looked hopeful.

'That would be terrific. We haven't actually booked a photographer, have we, Adam?' Gwen replied happily.

'I never gave it a thought. It's only going to be us at the ceremony, don't forget.'

Simone nodded.

'Of course. But it would be nice for you to have some reminders of your day. We could possibly print some out for the evening party.'

'I knew it was the right thing to do, getting in touch with you,' Gwen said to

Rory, smiling. 'Oh, isn't life good?'

'Well, we think so,' Rory agreed. 'In fact, we are planning to get married, too, quite soon. We hope you'll come over to France to be at our wedding.'

Adam was positively beaming.

'Congratulations!' he replied. 'That's terrific news, and of course we will come over to help you celebrate.'

★　★　★

The rest of the afternoon flashed by in a series of reminiscences. Frank came home and greeted the newcomers. Soon it was time for the two actors and Frank to leave for the hall.

'Can we come, too?' Simone asked. 'I can't wait to see the performance.'

'Of course you can. But I thought you might be too weary after your ferry crossing last night.'

'Not really.' Simone shook her head. 'I slept most of the time anyway. It would be good to see you both in action. I'm sure that tomorrow night we

226

can do something to help with the party?'

'Well, thank you.' Gwen smiled. 'There will be lots of things we haven't thought of. Let's go. I'll make sure you get good seats.'

Adam was thrilled to know his brother and partner were keen to see them in their roles and he hoped Simone would understand it all. Somehow, he seemed to have forgotten about his performance altogether and felt no nerves at all.

Gwen began to get her usual feelings of anticipation and was worried she had forgotten most of her lines, and even when she had to come on stage. She knew she would remember it all once she was in the dressing-room, but she really needed a few minutes' quiet to collect her wandering thoughts.

Was she really getting married tomorrow? She just had to get through this evening first, then somehow settle down to sleep. This was her last night as a single woman.

The seats in the hall weren't allocated so Rory and Simone found a seat near the front against the centre aisle. Adam thought that would be about the best place for them to sit — not too near the band but close enough to see all the action.

Mrs Probert had spent much of the first night grumbling about the band and the fact that her front row seat was not the best in the hall. The rest of the cast had all taken great delight in the fact that she wasn't happy and ignored her moans.

The rest of the audience had loved the music and clapped madly when Adam had sung with the band. He hoped it would be as enthusiastically received tonight.

He gave a little cough to clear his throat, hoping to goodness he wasn't getting a sore throat. Then he said goodbye to his brother and partner and went backstage to get ready.

If anything, it went even better the second night. The audience showed their pleasure at Adam's musical performance and clapped at every opportunity.

Marie and Sally played their parts with a touch of excellence that even Mrs Probert couldn't criticise. Even Geoffrey followed the script reasonably well.

Paul as Fairy Gok Mother went down a storm, and when Gwen was transformed to go to the disco, they audience roared their approval.

As they took their bows, Gwen looked at Adam and gave his hand a squeeze.

'Tomorrow,' she whispered.

He smiled at her as he took his bow.

The buzz in the dressing-room was enough to give anyone a headache as they chattered excitedly.

'Didn't it go well?' someone said.

'Amazingly,' someone else replied. 'I thought they weren't going to stop applauding at the end. I think Adam was the star of the show along with Gwen.'

'They make a lovely couple. When

are you going to get married for real?'

'Who can tell?' Gwen said, grinning.

'When are you going to make an honest woman of her, Adam?' Paul asked.

'Don't ask the impossible,' Adam teased. 'Excuse me. I need to go and find my brother and his partner.'

'You've got a brother?' Paul said in surprise. 'I never knew that.'

'Yes,' Adam replied. 'He's older than me and lives in France now. He and his partner have come over to stay with us for a few days.'

'I'd like to meet him. Will you invite him to the party after the show tomorrow?'

Adam nodded.

'Of course. We've actually invited several of our friends, but then we usually do.'

Gwen said nothing, knowing it was only a short while to wait till they made their announcement and they both wanted it to be a huge surprise to everyone.

'Are you ready, Adam?' she asked.

'I certainly am. Goodnight, everyone.'

There were calls of goodnight from around the room and they went through to the hall to find Rory and Simone. They were trapped in a corner talking to — or rather being talked at — by Mrs Probert.

'It's a pity you had to see everyone in such a pathetic performance,' she was saying. 'Not at all our usual sort of thing.'

Rory and Simone frowned.

'We loved it,' Rory argued. 'I thought Adam's singing was particularly good, didn't you?'

'I can't think why they had to bring in such a noisy group. It quite spoiled it for me and my friends.'

'So why did you come on both nights?' Rory asked innocently.

'Well, I'm usually in charge of front of house. I have to be here.'

'Really? Well, if you'll excuse us, my brother is coming out from backstage.'

'Your brother?' Mrs Probert probed.

'Adam Jerrold. I'm Rory Jerrold. Good evening.' He walked away with Simone holding his hand, leaving Mrs Probert standing open-mouthed.

'And what have you been saying to our dear Mrs Probert?' Adam asked with a grin.

'Just singing your praises. I gather she isn't your greatest fan?' Rory asked and Adam laughed.

'She dislikes everyone, I think. I'm surprised she actually turned up again. Anyway, what did you think?'

'Brilliant,' Simone enthused. 'I thought you were all very professional and it was a slick show with lots to entertain everybody.'

'Well, thank you.' Gwen was surprised at the warmth in her future sister-in-law's voice. 'We should get you to do the press report.'

'She's done some journalism, so she could well do it,' Rory told them. 'How about if she wrote a letter to the paper extolling the virtues of theatre in England?'

'Excellent idea!' Gwen smiled. 'Come on now. Let's get you home. You must be exhausted.'

'I do feel tired,' Rory admitted and Simone nodded her agreement. 'We all need to be wide awake tomorrow morning. What time is the wedding?'

'Shush. One never knows who is still listening,' Gwen said, indicating Mrs Probert who was still standing quite close.

Rory murmured his apologies as they all left the hall.

Back at Gwen's house, everyone said their goodnights and Adam went outside with Gwen.

'This will be the last time I say goodnight like this. Tomorrow, you'll be with me for the rest of our lives.' He kissed her forehead. 'Sleep well and I'll see you at the registry office tomorrow.'

'Goodnight, my love.'

'Goodnight.'

★　★　★

Adam was woken the next morning by his phone ringing.

'Mr Jerrold? Sergeant Chadwick speaking.'

Adam sat up, wide awake in seconds.

'It's about your car and that of Miss Harper,' the officer continued. 'It seems we've caught the perpetrators. Do you know Rocky Jones or Crystal Parkinson?'

'I know Crystal. Do you think she was involved?'

'It was her boyfriend. I gather they've been going around together for a while, unknown by her father. He seems a nice enough chap, but his daughter's been left to her own devices for a long time and has mixed with a few undesirables, including this Rocky character.

'We now have evidence to arrest and convict the pair of them. They took your car when they were under the influence of alcohol. Apparently, Miss Harper's car was taken to punish her. Something about some play or other and losing her part?'

'Heavens!' Adam replied. 'We suspected she might have had something to do with it, but we didn't have any proof. Do you know where Gwen's car might be?'

'I'm afraid we haven't found it yet,' Sergeant Chadwick said. 'I'm assuming she's got a hire one on her insurance?'

'Well, not yet. We've been busy with the play ever since. I think the chaps who took it actually threatened Gwen in the pub one night. Probably this Rocky was one of them.'

'Can I come round to see you this morning?' the sergeant asked. 'Some paperwork needs your signature.'

'I'm sorry but I'm rather busy today. The play, you know. We have a matinee performance this afternoon and I have plans for this morning.'

'I'll see you on Monday then, assuming you'll be around?'

'That's fine. Thanks very much.'

Adam switched his phone off and lay back. Why did everything always happen at once?

15

Something to Treasure

For the first time since Adam had proposed to her, Gwen was suffering from nerves. She was glad to have Simone with her, who seemed very calm and organised. Gwen was usually pretty laid back but today she fussed around getting breakfast and doing unnecessary things.

'Oh, dear,' she fretted. 'I've only got two sorts of cereal. I never thought about getting anything different.'

'Please don't worry,' Simone reassured her. 'I usually have toast and Rory will eat anything you put in front of him. I'm sure you have some cereal he will like.

'Now, why don't you sit down and eat something? You've got a busy day ahead. Sit down quietly and eat a decent breakfast. Shall I boil you an egg?' she offered.

'Oh, no. I should be doing it for you.'

'Sit down. I'm here to spoil you a little. It's very good of you to have put us up.'

They chatted easily and Gwen felt very pleased to have her as a sister-in-law. It was obvious, too, that Simone felt the same way.

Rory came downstairs and asked if there was some coffee.

'Help yourself. It's in the pot beside the cooker. Don't let Gwen wait on you. She's about to become a bride and needs to relax. We've got a couple of hours before she needs to be ready. What about you? What are you going to do with yourself?'

'I thought I'd go over to Adam's flat,' Rory replied. 'I can be some support to him.'

'Good idea.'

'I'll take my suit with me and go to the registry office with him. Then we'd like to take you out for lunch,' Rory addressed Gwen. 'I know it has to be quick, so perhaps you can suggest somewhere to go.'

Rory seemed to be very much in control and Gwen knew he'd be exactly the right person to be with Adam.

'Thank you. The matinee starts at two-thirty so a quick lunch would be perfect. There is food we could eat here, but going out would be much more interesting.'

Gwen was beginning to feel nervous again and wondered why. She swallowed hard as her phone rang.

'Oh, it's Adam. It isn't bad luck to speak to him, is it?' she asked in a panic.

'Of course not,' Simone assured her. 'Answer it.'

After she and Adam had discussed how much they were looking forward to the wedding, Adam updated her on the call he'd received from the police.

'They're ready to make some arrests for the theft of our cars. Crystal is involved. I just thought you might like to know. Are you OK?'

'I am. Rory's coming over to be with you. Dad can drive us over to the registry office then Rory wants to take us out for a quick lunch. Is that all right with you?' Gwen asked.

'That sounds excellent. I'll see you later. Bye, my love.'

Once Gwen had hung up the phone, Rory turned to her.

'You really do have a good relationship. I think you are perfect for each other.' He smiled at her and she touched his hand.

'Thank you. I'm so pleased you're both here with us to share the day.

'I'll get on my way,' Rory said. 'See you at half past eleven,' he said. 'Don't be late.'

$$\star \quad \star \quad \star$$

At Adam's flat, Rory was anxious to help.

'So what's on the to-do list?'

'We need to go to the baker's to

collect the food. I'll put what's necessary in the fridge and the rest will be fine. They'll be delivering the order to the hall as usual. Most people bring something themselves, too.'

'You really are quite the housewife, aren't you?' Rory teased. 'It's usually the women who do that sort of thing.'

'Don't forget I've been looking after myself for a good few years. We do it all between us. I don't believe in women's work and men's work.'

'Good idea. Who'd have thought the son of our parents would turn out so able? I think Mum would have been impressed.'

'And Dad would have been horrified.' Adam laughed as they gave each other a hug. 'I know I've said it before, but thank you again for coming over.'

'I wouldn't have missed it. I'm just so glad Gwen brought us together again.'

The morning passed by so quickly. It was soon time to dress for the wedding. The men looked handsome in their suits and Adam presented Rory with a matching tie.

'Goodness, I haven't put one of these on for a long time,' Rory commented.

⋆　⋆　⋆

Back at Gwen's home, she and Simone were getting ready, too. Gwen put on her new dress and, with trembling hands, fastened the belt.

She slipped on her new shoes and wished she'd actually worn them round the house. They felt rather uncomfortable and stiff. She looked at herself in the mirror and smiled happily.

There was a knock at her door.

'It's only me,' Simone called softly.

'Come in. I'm just about ready.'

'Oh, Gwen, you look gorgeous. What a perfect dress and it fits you so well.'

'You look lovely, too,' Gwen returned. 'That blue is so lovely. I think we shall certainly do our men proud. I'm going to wear this for the final wedding scene so when Adam announces it to the audience and company, I will be ready. I can't wait to see everyone's faces.'

'Your dad is downstairs ready and waiting,' Simone told her. 'I'm sorry I will be in the car with you both. It should be just the two of you.'

'Nonsense. It's all so informal, nothing has to be traditional. I'm delighted you're here with us.'

When Frank saw his daughter he had a tear in his eye which he wiped away, hopefully without them noticing.

'Are you both ready for this? Let's go then. I know you said no flowers but I wanted you to have something. I got this for you.'

He gave her a small box containing a necklace with a perfect flower made of a pearl surrounded by tiny diamonds.

'Oh, Dad, it's lovely!' Gwen exclaimed. 'Thank you so much. I will really treasure this.'

16

The Final Curtain

They set off and were soon parking outside the registry office. Adam and Rory were both already there, looking very alike in their dark suits and matching ties.

'I never realised they look so similar,' Simone muttered.

'Gwen, you look wonderful,' Adam said with a large lump in his throat. 'Perfect. You couldn't have chosen anything I liked more.'

He shook his head as if he couldn't believe this perfect vision was soon going to be his wife.

'Come on, then. Let's go in.'

They went inside and were soon ushered into the marriage room.

Twenty minutes later, they were Mr and Mrs Adam Jerrold.

They came out and stood on the steps for their photos to be taken by Simone.

'Congratulations to you both,' Frank said. 'I hope you'll be as happy as your mum and I always were.'

'Let's go and find some bubbly,' Rory suggested, 'and some food to mop it up.'

'I can't have too much to drink,' Adam reminded him.

'Nor me,' Gwen added. 'We've got a whole show to do this afternoon and again this evening.'

They went to a pub not far away and Rory ordered a bottle of champagne. Between five of them it disappeared rather quickly.

After a light lunch, they went home to change. Adam usually wore a leather jacket for the play and he decided to wear the same thing as usual to go to the hall.

Gwen changed into her jeans so no-one would have guessed what they'd spent the morning doing.

Rory and Simone were planning to bring their wedding finery to the evening performance, along with the food. It was all decided beforehand and gave the bride and groom nothing to worry about.

'Have you planned what you're going to say?' Gwen asked when they had arrived at the hall.

'I think so. Just a simple statement — we're now really married and this is our reception.'

'As long as the entire audience don't think it's a general invitation to stay!' she replied. 'We had better get ready now. Only one more performance before we make our announcement.'

Geoffrey arrived in the dressing-room looking as white as a sheet. He went into a corner and slumped down, looking totally defeated.

'What's up, Geoffrey?' one of the others asked.

'Private problems. I really would have preferred not to come here today but I felt I couldn't let you all down. Just leave me alone.'

Adam saw the encounter and knew exactly what had happened. He muttered something to Gwen about it and they both agreed to keep quiet about it.

Poor chap, she was thinking. His beloved daughter, Crystal, mixed up in so much trouble. He knew he had spoiled her all her life and this was the repayment he got.

She smiled at him gently and continued to get ready.

The afternoon matinee was full of children who all screamed and shouted at every opportunity. Most of the cast were used to this sort of behaviour and played up to the audience.

By five o'clock, the audience were all ready to leave the hall and the cast flopped down, feeling very weary.

'I'm getting too old for these matinees,' Paul groaned. 'I think next year we might give them a miss.

'Make sure that next time we do an unsuitable murder mystery,' he added bleakly. 'Anyone staying for tea?'

'We're going home for a break,' Adam told them. 'We have a few things to do.'

'You look excited,' Sally commented.

'Put it down to another good performance ticked off the list. Only one more to go.'

'Have you heard any more about your car?' she asked.

Adam glanced at Geoffrey, who was again slumped in the corner.

'I'll tell you later.'

Sally followed his look and suddenly twigged.

'Oh, dear,' she whispered. 'I'm so sorry. It must be awful for any parent to know that their child is involved in such goings-on.'

Adam nodded before he turned away.

'Are you ready?' Gwen asked.

They went back to Gwen's house and met the others. They all had a light tea and Simone produced a cake, so they all took a large slice.

'Now, then, let's get it straight,' she said in her best organising mode. 'We will collect all the food and put it in the back of our car, along with your suit and dress.'

'We can take the dry food in our car,' Adam said.

'All right. But you won't want to take your clothes for the finale. We can bring them round to the dressing-room before the finale so you can get ready. Then we'll unload the rest of the food and bring it on to the stage after everything has been cleared away. Right?'

'That sounds perfect. Thank you so much.' Gwen went over to kiss her. 'You are wonderful.'

'I'm really going to enjoy being a part of this family.'

'It's time we were going back,' Adam announced. 'Come on, Mrs Jerrold. Let's go and collect whatever it is we're taking this evening.'

They both laughed.

As always, the last night went very well with a few extras added. The band played well and Adam's solo with them was applauded and he even gave a short encore.

By the end of the final scene, excitement had risen to fever pitch in the hall. Even Geoffrey had relaxed a bit.

Then it was the wedding scene, traditional in all versions of 'Cinderella'.

The entire cast was waiting in the wings and went on stage in turn for their applause. Then, dressed in their finery, Adam and Gwen came on to the stage.

The cast all gasped when they saw the modern dress and suit. The audience cheered, not knowing anything was any different.

Adam stepped forward and raised his hand. The audience fell silent.

'Thank you all for giving us such terrific support this evening.' The cast applauded the audience. 'I feel this was a successful play which we wrote ourselves.'

Again, there was more applause.

'Today has been a special day for Gwen and me,' Adam continued. 'This morning, we were married and this is to be our reception.'

Everyone, including the cast, roared their approval.

Gwen and Adam stood in the midst of the throng, both of them near to tears. Paul then stepped forward and held up his hand for quiet.

'I think you've all made it clear that you approve. I'd like to offer our congratulations to the happy couple, on behalf of all of us. We wish you every happiness and we are cross you didn't tell us so we could buy you a present.'

There was much more applause and hugs from all those close enough to reach the happy couple.

A number of their friends and colleagues stayed behind to join the party.

'Oh, dear,' Marie moaned. 'I would have brought more salad if I'd known there would be more of us staying.'

'Don't worry,' Gwen told her. 'We've

got loads of extra food. My brother-in-law and his partner are bringing it in as we speak. And the bar is bringing in extra wine as well.'

The party was great fun with everyone enjoying the whole thing. But all too soon it was all over and they cleared the leftover food away.

'You know,' Adam said to his new wife, 'the best part of all of this, apart from the actual wedding itself, was you finding Rory and Simone. I'm so lucky to have him as a brother, and with such a lovely partner, too.'

Gwen smiled and leaned over to kiss her new husband.

Rory had heard what Adam had said and was quick to respond.

'Adam, I'm just so sorry to have lost touch with you for so long,' he confessed. 'It would never have happened if I'd known what I was missing.'

The two men, who seemed to look more and more alike as the night went on, gave each other a big hug.

Gwen smiled happily.

'Come on, then, husband, we need to go home now. You can see your brother again tomorrow.'

Hand in hand, the new bride and groom left the hall and went back to their home.

WHERE THE HEART IS
OUT OF THE BLUE
TOMORROW'S DREAMS
DARE TO LOVE
WHERE LOVE BELONGS
TO LOVE AGAIN
DESTINY CALLING
THE SURGEON'S MISTAKE
GETTING A LIFE
ONWARD AND UPWARD
THE DAIRY
TIME FOR CHANGE
BROKEN PROMISES

We do hope that you have enjoyed reading this large print book.

Did you know that all of our titles are available for purchase?

We publish a wide range of high quality large print books including:
Romances, Mysteries, Classics
General Fiction
Non Fiction and Westerns

Special interest titles available in large print are:
The Little Oxford Dictionary
Music Book, Song Book
Hymn Book, Service Book

Also available from us courtesy of Oxford University Press:
Young Readers' Dictionary
(large print edition)
Young Readers' Thesaurus
(large print edition)

For further information or a free brochure, please contact us at:
Ulverscroft Large Print Books Ltd.,
The Green, Bradgate Road, Anstey,
Leicester, LE7 7FU, England.
Tel: (00 44) **0116 236 4325**
Fax: (00 44) **0116 234 0205**

When troubled army veteran and musician Josh Robertson returns home to Nashville to be the best man at his younger brother Chad's wedding, he's sure that he's going to mess it all up somehow. But when it becomes clear that the wedding might not be going to plan, it's up to him and fellow guest Louise Giles to save the day. Can Josh be the best man his brother needs? And is there somebody else who is beginning to realise that Josh could be her 'best man' too?

FARMER WANTS A WIFE

Sarah Purdue

Skye works in London, with no intention of ever going back to the farming life in which she was raised. Then she travels to meet with Charles, a new client who lives in rural Wales. When she crashes her car in heavy snow, she is rescued by Ren and Gethin. Snowbound, she starts helping on their farm — and growing closer to Gethin. But when Skye's business with Charles threatens her new friends' livelihood, she has a hard decision to make . . .

ONE SUMMER WEEKEND

Juliet Archer

Alicia Marlowe's life as an executive coach is well under control — until she meets her new client, Jack Smith. Jack's reputation precedes him, and Alicia knows immediately that he spells trouble. Not least because he reminds her of someone else — a man who broke her heart and made her resolve never to lower her guard again. As long as she keeps Jack in his place, Alicia thinks she might just make it through unscathed. But Jack has other ideas — including a 'business' trip to the Lake District . . .